DAYS OF BLOODY THRONES

MATT LARKIN

DAYS OF BLOODY THRONES

Runeblade Saga: Book Two

MATT LARKIN

This is a work of fiction. Names, characters, organizations, businesses, places, events and incidents either are the product of the author's imagination or are used fictitiously.

Published by Incandescent Phoenix Books

mattlarkinbooks.com

CONTENTS

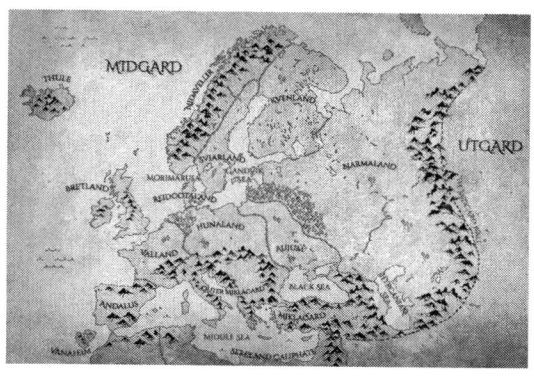

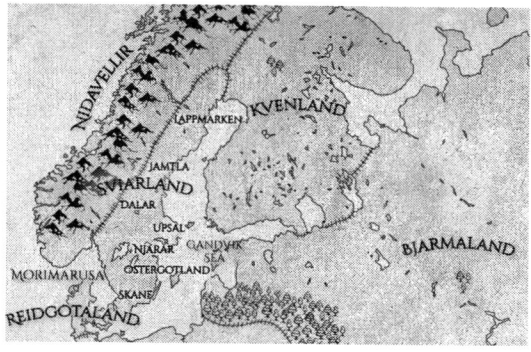

For more maps, join the Skalds' Tribe and get a free codex of
The Ragnarok Era:

https://www.mattlarkinbooks.com/go-runeblade/

PROLOGUE

A stream of shadows played around Volund's forge.

No mortal man ought to have treaded into this dverg ruin, far beneath the Sudurfells. Odin came here, though, from time to time, to check on the dark smith's progress. To remind the svartalf that, though Odin exhibited patience, it had limits. Besides which, Odin required a great many crafts from the smith.

Volund had forged one mighty weapon already for Odin, one that Thor put to good use ... or frequent use, in any event, and that served Odin's purpose well enough.

The beat of a hammer rang out through the workshop, echoing off ancient tunnels abandoned long ago. And now reclaimed by a being Odin could not quite understand. One could never fully trust an ally—if the term even applied— whom one did not understand. But still, no one else on Midgard could do what Volund did. His craftwork had become legend through the North Realms.

The man who forged a new runeblade, works once thought lost to history and even then, the sole province of the dvergar. A useful ally ... or a terrible liability.

The hammer crashed down on the anvil again, then stopped.

Volund could not have possibly heard Odin's silent approach into the forge, but he paused. Turned ever so slowly, exposing his ashen skin, his jet black hair. Fixing his unearthly gaze upon Odin even as his lip curled into that infuriating sneer.

"You know it will yet be some time before the next works are ready." The svartalf's voice was at once thick and etheric, as Otherworldly as the shadows that danced about him and his places, dimming Odin's torchlight and leaving the forge in near darkness.

Odin did not bother to answer the smith in any event. They both knew what Volund had promised him and how long it would take. The great and terrible crafts took years, and Odin had grudgingly learned patience. "You have proved very effective in arming my son, smith ... and still I failed to give proper consideration to yours."

Volund might have asked to which son Odin referred. But then, from the way he shook his head, limping over to a chair and sinking down into it, he knew well of whom Odin spoke.

Finally, settled down, Volund cleared his throat. "You did not come here to speak of Thor."

"Not this day, no."

"And Eightarms is no son of yours ... so what care you what use my son makes of him?"

Odin shrugged. "Starkad is not my son, true enough, but he is my ... emissary."

Volund chuckled, the sound mind grating, thick, and viscous in the air. "Does he know this? You send him to seek the lost runeblades of the Old Kingdoms ... Oh, yes, King of the Aesir. Did you think I would not take an interest in the greatest works of my former masters? In the very creations that inspired my own? If you intend to use Eightarms to claim those blades ... how are you to object if I wish to use him to reclaim my own creation?"

Odin leaned on Gungnir and fixed Volund with a level gaze. "Some years ago ..." Odin stared off into the flames of the forge, these too, seeming dim considering the heat of the blaze. "Some years ago, I called upon dark powers with which you are all too familiar on behalf of that boy. And I made him what he is, and thus, I made him mine."

Again, that horrid chuckle. "And men call me cruel. So, the very act with which you claim to have aided the man yet ensured he became your instrument. Driven endlessly to wander and seek out your prizes for you. I nearly wonder that you have not yet sent him to claim the other relics you require."

Yes, the blessing Odin had given Starkad all but ensured the man would continue to undertake his reckless quests. It did make him perfect for Odin's uses. And yes, Odin had suspected the end result when he'd called upon the Art. None of this was worth denying.

Instead, Odin paced around the forge, banging Gungnir's butt loudly on the ground with each step. "So be it, Volund," he said, at last, turning to see the smith still slouching in the chair. "I will not interfere with your plans for your son. I shall even allow him to call upon Starkad. But you ..." Odin pointed a finger at him. "Tread with care, svartalf. I claim that man in no uncertain terms, and I will not take kindly if you drive him on any path that interferes with my own intentions for him."

Another infuriating laugh. "You believe you alone are the master of urd, that you alone have the right to manipulate the actions of pawns on the board? Your own so-called friend Loki surely puts us both to shame with his machinations. You cannot play the game and demand no one else play it either."

Odin glowered at the smith. Part of him almost thought it might be better to strike Volund down, no matter how useful his crafts proved. But Odin needed him, needed his works, if he was to win Ragnarok. Needed Volund just as he needed Starkad and the damned runeblades.

"Do as you wish with your own pawns, your son included. But if you try to remove one of mine from the board before his time, our next conversation may prove unpleasant for us both."

"Oh ..." Volund rose, groaning ever so slightly with the effort. "And I do so enjoy these visits."

Grumbling, Odin slammed Gungnir on the floor one more time for good measure, then spun and stalked out of the workshop.

He had a great deal of work to do, and it seemed Volund would force him to watch his every move.

Because Volund was wrong about one thing ... Starkad was more valuable than any mere pawn. He was a piece Odin could not sacrifice until the time was right.

PART I

Third Moon
Year 28, Age of the Aesir
One Year After *Days of Endless Night*

1

*B*lood had crusted within the runes running along the length of the blade. It had drank deep, many a time, earning Hervor great renown, though more oft than not as Hervard, newest thegn to King Haki of Ostergotland.

She knelt by a stream, working the grime from the grooves with a fingernail. Always careful not to touch the blade's edge. One cut would kill like poison. Hervor had claimed her share of lives from mere nicks.

Her own blood trickled down beside her eye, and she had to wipe it away with the back of her hand. A hairsbreadth closer and that big fuck with the axe would have split her skull. As it was, he'd ruined her helm.

Over the course of the summer, Haki's fleet had raided throughout the Morimarusa, preying on Reidgotaland and islands nigh to Nidavellir. No man stood long against the runeblade Hervor bore. Tyrfing always claimed a life when drawn. Such was its curse.

With a sniff, Hervor rose from the stream, then wiped the blade dry. The runeblade would never rust and needed no sharpening, but still she thought it best to treat it with respect. It was, after all, her father's legacy. She saw to it first. Tonight, she'd deal with the gash above her brow.

Bodies littered the shore downstream. The men had resisted. Fools. After seeing their men cut to pieces, the women and children had surrendered. They now knelt in the bloody muck that had become the village grounds.

King Haki himself tromped amongst them, inspecting his new slaves. Raiding into Njarar had been bold, like to start a war even. But then, King Otwin's best days were long behind him now, and few would want to challenge Haki's might. He was collecting champions from among the North Realms, and Hervor was more than proud to count herself among them.

"Hervard," Haki said as she drew nigh. The king knew the truth about her sex, of course. Her grandfather was a jarl under Haki, after all, and she had gone to Haki's service with his blessing. Still, he let her have her disguise. Men were more like to fear the man wielding the runeblade than the shieldmaiden. Men were morons, of course. "Folke caught a wandering skald among these people."

"In this little village?"

"Fled from Upsal."

Hervor frowned. The Yngling kingdom … yes. A year in service to Haki had won her fame, wealth, a hoard to bury for her next life. It had not yet, however, brought her much closer to vengeance upon the Ynglings. Kings Yngvi and Alf —the whole fucking dynasty, in fact—had yet to pay for the death of her family. Oh, but they would. As Haki amassed champions, Hervor gathered allies, men who would follow her into battle.

Not that Haki needed to know aught of her plans. He was a means to an end. She shrugged, trying to seem unconcerned. "Why would a skald flee the court—"

"Of the most powerful kingdom in Sviarland?" Haki finished. "Because those fool brothers have gone and killed each other, just like their parents." He chuckled. "Fought over Yngvi's wife, the skald says."

Now Hervor faltered, her mouth hanging open. That was not how she'd expected this to go. "Wha ..." She shut her mouth. Well, fuck. She couldn't have vengeance on two dead kings.

Haki chuckled again, then moved on to inspect a slave woman, turning her chin this way and that. "This is why brothers ought to have *different* kingdoms. Some things are best not shared." He pinched the slave woman's cheek. "At least until one is done with them."

Did the king think to get a rise out of Hervor? If so, he would be disappointed. So Yngvi and Alf were dead now ... her oath was to bring down the Yngling dynasty. "Who has claimed the throne?"

"The skald didn't know. The craven fled the kingdom when the brothers' followers set to fighting one another. Here he thought Njarar to be safer." Haki grinned. "There's no safe in the North Realms."

No, and Haki was fast becoming the most infamous raider throughout. Only Dalar and Upsal truly matched his power, and Upsal was vulnerable.

"Both Yngling kings had sons, yes?" Hervor said, following the king as he headed back toward their ship.

"So I've heard. Probably killing one another now."

"And while they do so, Upsal is weak." Under Yngvi and Alf, some called Upsal the strongest of the kingdoms of Sviarland. But now ...

"We think alike, Hervard. Now's the time for a raid, even late as the summer grows. We can sail around Njarar and strike hard."

"No."

The king had been about to jump in a boat to row back to the longship. Now he stopped, then turned back to her. "No?"

"No, I was not thinking of a raid. I was thinking of conquest."

⚓

HAKI'S BROTHER Hagbard lounged over the throne in Haki's hall when Hervor and the king entered. The king scoffed at his brother but did not chide him. Perhaps Haki was right— without shared kingship, they lacked the rivalry that had brought down Yngvi and Alf.

"The scouts you requested returned not an hour ago," Hagbard said. "They confirm what the craven skald has told you."

That very skald—Knut—stood in the hall now. Haki had forced the man to wear a woman's dress whenever he recited poetry, which Hagbard demanded almost nightly. Folke, one of Haki's other champions, heckled the skald while flinging bits of grease at the fool. The oaf would tire of the game soon enough, Hervor supposed, and then the skald was like to wind up dead. Cravens deserved no better.

Haki settled into a chair at the head of the largest table. "The kings of Upsal are dead."

"Indeed. And Ochilaik has now claimed the throne. The young sons of Yngvi have fled Upsal."

Hervor sat to the king's right, nodding at the other thegns as she joined them. Kare returned her nod, but Folke was too caught up with tormenting Knut. Hervor looked to Haki. "Then we ought to find it a simple matter to strike now, before he has time to consolidate his power."

"Ah, that." Hagbard shrugged. "Too late. He's already hired not only Geigad but also Svipdag of Lappmarken to guard his new throne. To say naught of the other mercenaries."

"Fuck," Haki mumbled.

Kare snarled and spit while Folke groaned.

"It seems we are back to mere raids then," Hagbard said.

"*No*," Hervor said. Not now. Not when she'd been so close to annihilating the whole damned dynasty. "No, we can still do this."

The king scowled. "Bring some mead!" He took a long swig of the drinking horn the moment a slave brought it, then tossed it aside. "Great as our champions may be, Hervard, few men are more famous at arms than Svipdag. Even if we took the throne, the cost in lives would make it hard to hold."

She leaned forward, pressing on the table. She was not going to let it end like this. "Few men are so famed, true. But I know of one even more famed."

Hagbard snorted. "Would you have us hire Tyr himself?"

"Starkad Eightarms."

At that, everyone at the table looked to her. Even Folke broke his taunts and stared open-mouthed at her.

Finally, Haki spoke. "The man has fought for the Ynglings oft over the years."

She shook her head. "His loyalty is to silver, same as any mercenary. And he knows me; we fought together. We were ... friends." Was that a stretch? Perhaps. They had saved each other's lives, though, and that counted a great deal. At least she thought it did.

Haki rubbed his beard. "Silver we have aplenty after so many raids. If he will join and lead my champions, I'd gladly pay him his weight in it."

"Let me offer him more. Twice his weight, even." Starkad was worth it. Hervor had never seen a man faster with a blade.

Haki looked to Hagbard, who shrugged. "So be it," the king said. "Go and find Starkad, and carry our offer to him. And do so swiftly."

2

*A*s winter drew closer, the mountains of Njarar became more and more inhospitable. In such perilous heights rose the castle of King Otwin, son of the long-dead Nidud, famed for his cruelty. In the town below the mountains, Starkad stood on a bridge, staring up at those mountains, torch held out to his side. Below him plunged a waterfall that might soon freeze over.

Before the rise of the Old Kingdoms, dvergar built that fortress. Decades ago, Nidud had claimed the place and the riches within and built up his petty kingdom with it. Ominous and dark, the fortress rose above the mist, a fell peak atop the mountains. Climbing such slopes, assaulting the hold, would prove a challenge even for the likes of the Aesir.

But then, Starkad could never shy away from a challenge.

Wudga sauntered up beside Starkad and leaned against the bridge rail. "If we are to do this, we ought to do so before winter settles in."

Starkad shrugged. "As long as you are paying, we can go

where you wish, when you wish." He turned away from the rail to look at the man now beside him. Wudga had eyes so dark they seemed nigh to black. His hair was dark brown, but in the twilight, even that seemed black. He looked a man in his mid-twenties, but Starkad had known him decades ago, and Wudga had changed almost as little as Starkad himself. At least outwardly. "I have to ask though—and it matters naught, I'd aid you either way—but are your claims mere pretense to take the throne?"

Wudga scowled, a look so dark Starkad could almost have sworn it hastened the fall of night. "I do not seek the throne, nor care much for the fate of Njarar."

"But you said you were the son of Princess Bodvild, yes? Otwin's own nephew?"

"You have a long memory." Wudga sniffed. "My father sends me to complete his vengeance and claim his legacy. Naught else here concerns me overmuch."

His father. According to Wudga, he was the son of Volund himself. The legendary dark smith who had wrought vengeance upon Nidud beyond the pale of what men could imagine. Moreover, Volund had crafted a new runeblade, the only such not made by the dvergar.

And here Starkad was, about to let another of the damned things go. Let Wudga claim it, as he had let Ecgtheow do so. That loss haunted Starkad's dreams. It sent him skittering awake as though a serpent nested down with him. He ought to have claimed the runeblade of Thule for himself instead of letting Gylfi's thegn take it. The mistake had tormented Starkad nigh to every night since.

And he was about to repeat it.

He swallowed. Sometimes he wondered, did his dreams of finding another runeblade come from his own cursed nature, or did Odin so prompt him? In the end, it mattered little. In either case, he could not long deny his need. And yet, Wudga had hired him solely to help him claim his legacy. Starkad could not well betray such trust, nor so old a friendship.

He had … so few friends left.

With a grunt, Starkad spat over the rail into the mist above the falls. "Unless you plan to raise an army, we must rely on stealth to assassinate Otwin."

"Indeed. I see no alternative but to—"

The bridge creaked as another crossed onto it, obscured by the mist. Starkad jerked his torch out in front of him to dispel the vapors. Night was already settling in, and most townsfolk should have locked themselves in their homes by now, justly fearing the mists.

The man striding toward them was no native, though, but a warrior, clad in chain and bearing a sword over his shoulder. One of Otwin's soldiers. No surprise, given their proximity to the king's castle.

Starkad reached for one of the swords on his back. Wudga too had a hand on his blade.

The approaching warrior removed his—*her*—helmet.

Starkad faltered. "Hervor?"

"You know her?" Wudga asked.

Starkad nodded, not quite certain what to say. He might ask what the woman was doing here. He supposed.

Hervor beat him to it. "I've been searching for you the better part of a moon."

"Why?"

She glanced around, then drew very nigh to his side. "I have work for you."

Now he snorted and shook his head. "Even did I not have a prior engagement, you could not afford me."

"King Haki can." She looked to Wudga. "You trust this man?"

Starkad shrugged. "Wudga, I will join you in the lodge soon. Give us a moment."

The other man frowned and with it, the shadows seemed to grow deeper. Damned unnerving, that, and aught Starkad had remembered about him long winters back. Finally, Wudga nodded, then strode back the way Hervor had come.

"It's good to see you," she said.

Starkad nodded. Still uncertain what to say. What did she mean by that, anyway? A man could never trust a woman. Ogn had taught him that and taught him so well he was never like to forget.

Though ... Hervor *had* fought by his side and fought damned well. So ... maybe he could trust her a *little*. At least in battle. "I ... what is this about King Haki?"

"Haki of Ostergotland."

"I know *who* he is. I mean, what work does he offer?"

Hervor looked around again, looking over the edge of the falls. Did it remind her of going over those falls in Thule? Did she fear that? "This place looks not unlike the realm of Hel."

"We've seen other places more like Niflheim than this, you and I."

She grimaced. "Yngvi and Alf are dead."

"So I heard." It grieved him, a little, though the brothers had been but a shadow of the greatness of their fathers, Alrik and Eirik. In any event, he owed them no special loyalty save at times when they hired him.

"Alf's son Ochilaik has turned on his cousins and claimed the throne. Haki thinks to take it for himself and from there, perhaps to claim rulership over all Sviarland."

Starkad scoffed at that. "I rather think Gylfi might have something to say on the matter." Other kings might prove a threat to Haki—Siggeir Wolfsblood, perhaps—but no one could deny the influence the sorcerer King Gylfi wielded as the voice of Odin. Gylfi was the most feared king in Sviarland and with good reason.

"Gylfi grows ancient. In any event, that matters naught. First, Haki turns his sights on Upsal."

Now Starkad shook his head and leaned against the rail. "You'd have me act against the grandson of Alrik? I was … fond of the man." In younger days, Starkad had barely been a man back then, and already he had lost much. Alrik had given him a purpose, at least until he and Eirik had slain one another. He might not have owed the Ynglings loyalty— but he still didn't see himself killing Alrik's own blood without a damned good reason.

"Ochilaik is *not* his grandfather. Besides, Haki will pay you."

"No."

Hervor moved closer, until he could feel her breath on his face. "Twice your weight in silver."

The mere sound of it stirred something in his gut. So much wealth … it would not satisfy him. He knew that. And yet … Hel, he wanted it. Always more. Starkad worked his jaw a moment. "So much?"

"Haki has grown wealthy … and has no hesitation to share his good fortune with his allies."

Damn it.

Damn, but Alrik and Eirik were long dead. Like the past.

Like so many people Starkad had known … his mother, his—the man he once believed his father. Vikar. Bragi. Even Orvar-Oddr. So many friends lost. Naught truly lasted. "I'll do it. First though, I must fulfill my current employment."

Hervor grumbled something under her breath. "Which is?"

"To kill a king."

Hervor now looked up to the fortress in the mountains, though with night fallen, Starkad could no longer make out its outline. The woman glowered a bare moment, then tapped the golden hilt of her runeblade. "Well, then. Let us be about it."

3

A freezing wind swept over the mountain and blasted Hervor in the face, prickling her exposed skin and chilling her even beneath her layers of armor. Yes, this place seemed not so very unlike the horrors they had experienced in Thule. As with then, they moved in the night, ascending a steep path and barely able to see their own godsdamned feet.

This path ran up the side of the mountains toward Otwin's fortress, but the walkway was narrow enough every one of them preferred to move single file. Actually, Hervor would much have preferred not to have come at all, certainly not now.

She hated moving at night.

It was mist-madness at its finest.

At best, you'd slip and break your damned ankle. At worst ... Hervor paused a moment to peer over the precipice a mere foot to her left. Naught but mist and a fall into darkness.

One such fall had been more than enough for her lifetime.

Already, ice crusted the sharp rocks along the slope, as if unable to wait for the proper onset of winter. It made everything slicker, more treacherous.

Starkad led the way, followed by his employer, this Wudga, a man who seemed too fell himself. He'd already probably spent too long out in the mists. Wudga had three men with him, mercenaries, two of which he'd allowed to carry torches. No more, claiming the lights might reveal them, even through the mist.

True enough, but it hardly mattered if they died upon these slopes.

Starkad coughed and turned back to their small party. "If we continue this way, we'll reach the main gate."

"They'll shoot us down before we're halfway up," Wudga said.

Starkad nodded, then patted the jagged rock face that flanked the path. "We are but six men ..." He glanced at Hervor. "Six warriors against a small army. So the clearest path to victory seems to enter from the rear of the castle, the unguarded side from which our foes imagine no enemy might approach."

"Wait," Hervor said. "You want to climb the fucking cliff?"

"Unless you can fly like a valkyrie, I see no alternative."

Hervor spat into the mist. "Every time I go anywhere with you ..." She flung her pack down on the rocks, then began digging through it for the damned crampons. Last time, she wound up with these climbing spikes tearing up her back, thanks to Bragi Bluefoot. Poor old bastard. She hoped Odin had taken the skald in at Valhalla. "Doing this in darkness will get us all killed."

Starkad grunted, then kicked at the ice with his own crampon. Without further answer, he heaved himself upward, ascending with almost frightening speed. Damn but he was strong.

Wudga followed while one of his mercenaries grumbled about having to hold a torch while climbing.

Hervor sympathized. "Go ahead and put it out, then. I mean the mist will eat our memories and feast on our souls, but your life will be easier for an hour or so." So she sympathized a little.

With that, she kicked the rock face herself, scraping until her foot found purchase, then hefting herself upward. The ice-crusted rocks were slick. Kept trying to slip out from under her fingers. Ten feet up and her fingers felt like they'd be falling off from frostbite.

Hel damn Starkad to the wastes of Niflheim for this.

Fifty feet or so up, a rock broke away under her weight and plummeted down below.

Hervor threw herself against the cliff. Her foot skidded, her crampons threatening to pull free from their purchase.

From below, one of the mercenaries sputtered curses about the falling rock.

Panting, Hervor cast a glance up above. She couldn't see five feet, damn it. All the light was below her.

"Starkad!"

A fell wind whipped against her.

"What?" the call came a moment later.

"We cannot see!"

Again a pause.

"I can't exactly light a fucking torch while clinging to the cliff!" And the voice came from even farther above than before.

Well, fuck him too.

Grunting with the effort, Hervor pulled herself up again. And again. Just keep going.

Her arms ached from the effort. The cold seared her lungs with each painful breath. But she could do this.

Thule had been worse than this. This she could manage. At least there were no draugar here to—

A shriek rang from below, and the torchlight disappeared into the mist.

"Medard!" one of the mercenaries below her shouted. "Med!"

Fuck.

Hervor blinked, desperately trying to adjust her eyes to the now deeper darkness that had engulfed them. At least there had been light below them before. Now, thanks to poor dead Medard, she could not make out aught.

"Hervor!" Starkad shouted from far above. "I found a ledge. Wait and I'll light a torch!"

Wait, he said. What other godsdamned choice did she have? Climb blindly? Odin's balls.

Pressed up against the frozen rocks, every heartbeat seemed to stretch on forever. She had to get her breathing under control. Panic would kill you faster than aught else.

Hervor clinched her teeth. Blinked again. Once more. A hint of moonlight pierced the mist, almost unnoticeable until you found yourself with no other light.

A tiny flicker of flame sprung to life above her. Hard to judge the distance ... thirty feet up? Hervor blinked again, focusing on the cliff, not the light. Staring at it would make her night vision worse. Just pull up. One hand above the next.

Now her foot. Climb. Find her footing.

Climb.

And breathe. Steady breaths.

The remaining pair of mercenaries were still cursing below, but Hervor tried not to listen. Couldn't afford distractions. A shadow loomed above her. The overhang of a ledge. After pulling herself up as close as possible, Hervor had to lean back, slapping the edge of the overhang with one hand. There was no way she'd be able to pull herself up at this angle, was there?

No, she'd have to come at this from the side and then—

An iron grip wrapped around her wrist and yanked her upward. Starkad caught her in his arms an instant later, then pulled her up to the ledge. The whole space was narrow, not more than five feet on a side, but it dipped back into the cliff a few feet too. A hint of shelter against the bitter, merciless wind.

The torch lay on the ground. Hervor scrambled over too it, holding her freezing fingers so close to the flame they stung. Starkad eased her away by the shoulder, then snatched up the torch and leaned over the ledge with it, shining light for those climbing below.

Well, she could hardly complain about that. She fucking wanted to, but she couldn't rightly do so.

Instead, she crawled over as close to the wall as she could get. Wudga crouched there, not looking half so cold or miserable as she felt. Nor even over-bothered by the darkness or mist. What kind of man didn't fear the night? But then, she'd answered that already. A mist-mad man feared naught. Was that what had happened to Wudga?

"You stare at me."

Hervor jerked at his words. She fished around for an appropriate response, but naught came to mind.

"You think me odd, perhaps. A touch of something ... Otherworldly?"

Oh Hel. Was that what was wrong with this man?

She barely stilled the urge to grasp Tyrfing's hilt. Yes, she had seen those who had touched the Otherworlds. The

Niflungar sorcerers who had once pursued her for the runeblade she stole from their island. The likes of which she hoped never to lay eyes upon again. "You're a sorcerer."

Wudga snorted, then spat off into the mist. "Hardly. How many true sorcerers do you think walk Midgard? How many have you ever seen?"

Two, and that was two too many. Whatever they dealt in, it was foulness and unnatural, power seeming drawn from Hel herself.

Starkad heaved another man up on the ledge. This mercenary—panting and shivering—crawled over to where Hervor and Wudga crouched. With shaking fingers, he pulled a skin from his belt and drank deeply. Hervor shook her head.

Fool.

"There's more climbing ahead."

He gasped, breaking away from his drink a mere moment. "I'm freezing my fucking stones off, boy." And he took another long swig.

Hervor sneered at him. Let him drink himself stupid, then. Mead might make him warm for a moment, but it would also make him apt to slip on his climb. She just needed to make certain he was below her, not above.

Starkad helped the last of their party atop the ledge— now too crowded—then stalked over and snatched the mead skin away from the other mercenary. "Don't talk to Hervard that way."

Hervor snorted. "Like I need you to stand up for me."

Starkad tossed the skin to Wudga, who stuffed it in his pack. "Well, I didn't hear you standing up for yourself."

Because Hervor was just as happy to let the man who spoke thus get himself killed. A response she bit back. "This is your fool plan, Starkad. Already a man is dead."

"I did not hear you offer a better option."

Hervor chortled at that. "I offered you a fortune to fight for King Haki. That seemed a much better plan."

"And perhaps an oath already given means naught to you, but—"

She rose. "I know the value of an oath." More than he could ever imagine.

For her oath, she had murdered his friend, Orvar-Oddr. For her oath, she would yet destroy the Yngling dynasty, those Starkad had once served. She would break no oaths.

Nor could she ask Starkad to do so. That was why she had come up this damned mountain. So it was time to get this task done with.

A king still needed killing.

twin's castle lay high atop these mountains. Like his father, the king of Njarar, must have thought himself unassailable, hidden away in this dverg outpost. He was mistaken, of course. Any fortress could be breached, if a man had the courage, cunning, and speed to pull it off.

Starkad crested the top of the cliff, pausing on his knees to catch his breath. From here, the ground actually descended to the top of the castle. High windows looked up from the sloping roof, letting in the moonlight to whatever hall lay below. Smoke wafted out of those openings, no doubt from braziers below. The feast hall?

Towers flanked that part of the roof, probably guarded by archers, but they would be looking down at the path, not back into the mountains. Naturally, they'd assume the sheer cliff protected approach from any other side. A fair guess.

Most nights.

Wudga trudged over to join Starkad where he knelt. "I can almost taste the king's blood."

"Such talk makes you sound like a draug."

Wudga shrugged, then glanced back at the cliff face

where Hervor was just rolled up over the top. "I need you to hold off Otwin's warriors ... but the king himself is mine. I alone must finish what my father began nigh to five decades ago. I will bring an end to this entire cursed bloodline."

Starkad rose, with a grim nod. He did not bother to point out that, as the son of Otwin's sister, Wudga himself continued the bloodline. Perhaps he considered Volund's blood so much the stronger as to render his other half moot. Starkad could empathize with a man who tried to deny his own parentage.

Panting, Hervor stumbled over to them. "Fuck you both ... for this plan ..."

Wudga looked the shieldmaiden up and down a moment like he actually considered laying with her.

It went on long enough Starkad scowled. "Come. The other two approach."

As Hervor had predicted, Reinhard looked a bit worse for his drink, chest heaving and face flush. Not that Ewald looked so very much better off. Nor any of them, Starkad supposed.

He glanced up at the sky. The night had drawn on, and dawn lay but a few hours away. They needed to do this before anyone in that castle began to wake. That meant they had no time to rest here.

With a nod at the others, Starkad took off down the steep incline. His feet skidded on the snow, and he did not fight it. His momentum carried him toward the castle's sloping roof as though he wore skis. As he drew nigh, a problem became apparent. There was a drop between the mountainside and the castle roof of a dozen feet. Deep in winter, the snows might have piled over and eliminated the issue.

Now, Starkad could not halt his momentum. Instead, at the edge, he jumped.

For an agonizing heartbeat, he flew through the air. Then he hit the stone roof, landed with a roll, and took a heavy impact on his shoulder. His swords clattered against the ice-crusted stonework. Starkad skidded along it, rolling back toward the mountain before he finally managed to catch himself. Less graceful and far more noisy than he might have hoped.

Through a wooden roof, they'd surely have heard him, but dverg-wrought stone ... perhaps not.

Wudga landed on the roof an instant later, before Starkad had even managed his feet. Hervor and the other two came up right behind the man. Reinhard failed to jump at all, and instead pitched off and slammed hard into the roof. The man lay very still.

Hel take that imbecile. Starkad stalked over and prodded him.

Dead, his neck broken.

Damned drunkard. Now they were down two men, and they hadn't even engaged the enemy. Wudga's plans had not accounted for foolery on the part of his own mercenaries ... could they still pull this off?

Grumbling, Starkad left the body where it lay and crept over to one of those high windows. Hervor joined him, and they peered down. The windows did indeed overlook a feast hall, and though the room stood empty, the drop had to be twenty feet down. Why did the dvergar feel the need to build things so damned big? They themselves were shriveled wrecks of men's bodies.

Nor was there any obvious spot on which to secure a rope up here.

Hervor pointed through the window to iron-plated

rafters that supported the feast hall. "We could reach those through the other window," she whispered. "But we'd have no means of retreat if ..."

"If things turn against us?" He shrugged. He had not come here to retreat. He crept over to the window she had indicated. She was right. They could make the jump down to the rafters and then from there to the floor, hopefully without breaking any bones.

Starkad rubbed his hands together and waited until the others had drawn up behind him.

Ewald scoffed at the sight. "You're fucking jesting with me."

"So stay up here until summer, then," Wudga said.

Starkad smirked. Right. They didn't really have much choice at this point.

The window was not so very tall, forcing him to make an awkward, crouching jump. The one time the dvergar did *not* build large—probably wanted to minimize the risk of sunlight. Starkad leapt forward, fell, and slammed hard into the rafter. His momentum pitched him forward, and he slipped, falling again. He wrapped both hands around the beam as he fell, catching himself. There, he hung, one hand on each side of the rafter.

Not much chance of pulling himself back up. So naught to do except drop. He looked down. A dozen feet. Or more. It wouldn't kill him, but that did not look enjoyable. But then again, he wanted adventure.

He wanted to know his limits. And surpass them.

Exhaling, Starkad released the beam and fell. He landed in a crouch, hoping to lessen the impact. It still stung his ankles, and a grunt escaped him. Slowly, he rose, drawing both swords as he did so. Above him, Hervor dropped onto the rafter, not repeating his mistake.

A glance around. No one coming.

"Wait," he whispered up at her. He placed his swords upon a table, then held out his arms. No sense in her hurting herself as well.

Hervor frowned, as if uncertain.

"Jump!" he snapped as quietly as he could.

With a grunt, she did. Starkad caught her, but her weight bore them both down. She landed atop him, lay there for a bare instant, then scrambled off him. Before Starkad had even risen, Wudga leapt down beside them.

Starkad got up and held out his arms for Ewald. The man scowled, shaking his head.

"You have nowhere else to go," Starkad said.

Grumbling, Ewald dropped off the beam. Starkad caught him too, this time better braced, and managed to keep his feet.

Wudga stalked closer to the main gate that seemed to lead into the great hall. Starkad retrieved his blades, then crept up beside his employer. In the other room, four groggy guards leaned against the wall, muttering to one another. A number of passages led out of that hall.

"Which way?" Starkad whispered.

Wudga pointed to one. "The king's chambers lie through there."

Starkad wanted to ask how the man knew with such certainty, but this was neither the time nor place for such questions.

"You and Ewald take the guards," Wudga said. "Block that passage against reinforcements." He drew his own sword. "I'll take the shieldmaiden in case any other guards protect the king."

Starkad glanced at Hervor, who nodded. She did bear the runeblade ... and of course, holding off the army in a corridor was a task only Starkad could do. So why did he hesitate to send Hervor alone with Wudga?

No, better not to dwell on doubts. Better to charge out there, slay his foes, and be done with it. He exchanged a nod with Ewald, then raced forward, swords bared.

A disbelieving shout went up while he was still twenty feet from the guards. They fumbled with halberds, slowed by fatigue or drink or both. By the time he'd reached them, they had leveled the weapons. A gray-haired man thrust at him. Starkad beat the shaft away with one sword, then stepped inside the man's reach so he could knock aside the halberd of another foe.

A third man rushed off to engage Ewald.

Perfect.

Gray-Hair tried to grab him. Starkad jerked a pommel up into the man's jaw, staggering him. Poor bastard stumbled backward even as Starkad thrust the same sword forward, impaling the other halberdier. A third man came in swinging hard.

Starkad jumped backward, out of reach, and the halberd bit into the shoulder of the guard he'd already impaled. He couldn't miss this chance ... Starkad lunged forward, swinging both blades in a whirl. The guard jerked his halberd up, managed to block one blade on the haft and fall back out of range of the other. Again and again, he parried Starkad's furious blows.

The guard was fast.

Starkad was faster.

He scraped a sword along the halberd shaft, drawing it down. Drawing the man's attention. A quick swipe of his other sword sheared through the guard's cheek and collided with his helm. A blow like that didn't need power to seriously distract and slow a man. Starkad spun, cutting out the guard's throat with his other blade.

Gray-Hair had risen, blood streaming down from a busted nose and the guard of his helm bent out of position. He charged forward, thrusting the halberd. Starkad twisted out of the way and cut him down too.

Ewald had felled his guard too, though it had earned him a wicked cut running from his jowls, over his neck, and into a shoulder. The mercenary was coughing, spitting blood.

"Move!" Starkad shouted, no longer bothering with stealth.

Hervor and Wudga had already vanished down the corridor. And it fell to him and Ewald to guard that passage as long as needed.

5

A shout echoed down the corridor as Hervor chased after Wudga. The guards might not have known what was about, but they knew trouble had landed in their midst. Just not how much.

Starkad's employer dashed around a corner and up a flight of stairs.

The man knew exactly where he was going. Had he been here before? How else would he know this castle's layout?

At a landing atop the stairs, a pair of guards blocked the way, here favoring broadswords instead of halberds. Wudga paused, glancing from one to the next and waving his axe around in slow circles.

Footfalls resounded on the stairs below them. Either some men had gotten past Starkad—unlikely as that sounded—or a few had come from the adjoining corridors. Didn't matter. They had little time.

Tyrfing in hand, Hervor turned back to the stairs even as a new pair of warriors crested onto the landing. "Do what you came to do!" she shouted at Wudga.

The first of her attackers lunged in, making wild sweeps

with that blade. Clearly intent to cleave her in half. Thinking her smaller, weaker. Hervor stepped into a swing, parried, and riposted. Tyrfing darted inside the man's guard and tore through his mail like he wore naught but cloth. The warrior fell back, blank stupidity on his face.

Dumb shit didn't know he was already dead.

Wound would fester and eat away at him like poison. Tyrfing always stilled at least one heart.

The other man advanced with more measured paces, tried to circle her. Not happening. Hervor feinted to his left, then jerked Tyrfing back, low. Her runeblade sheared through the man's knee and sent him tumbling to the ground, screaming in agony she could barely imagine.

"What the ..." the first warrior said, gaze locked on Tyrfing.

Hervor raised it up, turning the flat of the blade so he could see the runes engraved along it, now filling with blood from her victims. He paled further, and that was all the chance she needed. Hervor charged him, and—in his shock —he failed to raise his own blade. Tyrfing punched through his jaw and out the back of his skull. Her victim's blood sprayed her. Stung her eyes. Got in her mouth.

Hervor spit and jerked the blade free.

The whole landing stank with death and guts. Coppery taste was in her mouth.

She turned.

Wudga's axe was embedded in one man's skull. He wrestled with the other, shoved him against the wall. They were grunting, each fumbling. Wudga wriggled one hand ever upward, toward the man's face. Finally, he got leverage and dug his fingers into the poor bastard's nostrils. The guard shrieked and writhed. It gave Wudga the chance to pull a knife. And then the blade was in the guard's gut.

Again and again Wudga punched the blade into his slowing victim. Finally, panting, he let the man fall, smearing a bloodstain on the back wall as the body slipped down.

Another man came tromping down the hall, this one clad in polished mail and a silvery crown. Bearing a blade that seemed to reflect the light from the sconces all wrong. Runes flickering.

Wudga stumbled away from the man he'd killed. "Otwin." He planted a foot on his first victim's chest, then heaved his axe free. The crunch of skull and brains that lurched out with the blade turned Hervor's stomach, despite her long years of violence. "I have come for my father's legacy." Wudga pointed that axe at the runeblade. "Hand over Mimung, and I will grant a swift death."

The aged king of Njarar sneered, advancing on them.

Hervor backed off to the side, flanking their foe. Just how powerful was this Mimung? It was not one of the original nine runeblades, true, but men claimed Volund was the greatest smith in Midgard. So was it a match for Tyrfing?

Wudga roared at the man, all animal fury and sounding much like a snow bear. He lunged forward with tight, powerful swings of that axe. Otwin fell back before Wudga. The king was old now. Getting slow. Wudga should have this in hand. If it was his vengeance, his family's vengeance, then Hervor ought to let him attend to it himself. It was what she'd have wanted if—

The king twisted in a tight riposte. Mimung sheared through Wudga's axe right on the blade, scored it down so far a huge chunk of it snapped right off. A twist of the sword sent the ruined weapon flying from Wudga's hand. Skittering along the stone floor.

Oh. Fuck.

Hervor raced forward, shoving Starkad's employer out of the way even as Otwin tried to skewer him with a thrust. If Mimung worked aught like Tyrfing, Wudga could not afford so much as a scratch from it. Hervor jerked Tyrfing up to parry. The impact echoed through the landing, and Otwin stumbled back, face slack. Not believing any weapon had stood up to his own? How many years had he wielded that thing?

Indeed, for that matter, should not this man have been past sixty winters? Approaching seventy? Few lived so long, much less still able to fight. Was that the sword affecting him? Hervor shook such musings from her mind as Otwin advanced again. *Not* the time.

The king cut, thrust, and attacked again and again. His breath came heavy, yes, but he had the speed of a man half his age. It was all Hervor could do to parry or dodge every blow. This man had clearly spent years upon years practicing with only this blade and had learned its weight so perfectly. She twisted Tyrfing, tried to riposte. Otwin moved faster, turned Mimung inside and jerked it down.

The runeblade cut through Hervor's mail and gouged her arm.

She faltered, fell back a step and stared at the wound.

No.

No!

It ... it didn't feel like poison. But then again, did a man struck by Tyrfing know himself damned?

She darted her gaze between the wound and the man who had dealt it. Fuck. And fuck him. If she was going to die, she'd take this bastard with her.

Wudga used the opportunity to charge in, now bearing a sword claimed from a dead guard. He swung with all the same fury he'd had with the axe. Strong. Fast. But not enough control. Not quite proper training.

Still. A smart warrior took every advantage.

Hervor raced in while Otwin engaged Wudga. She didn't swing for the king though but for his sword. Tyrfing clanged against Mimung once again, knocking it out of place as the king tried to parry Wudga's blade. The stolen sword crashed against the king's helm, sending the man staggering to his knees, the sound of it nigh to deafening, even to Hervor's ears.

Shrieking, she swept Tyrfing in a low arc. Her runeblade severed Otwin's forearm, and he crashed to the ground, his screams barely audible over the ringing in her ears.

Hand on her shoulder, Wudga shoved her away.

Hervor spat. Worked her jaw to clear her head. Let the man have his vengeance. It was one thing she understood only too well.

Wudga hefted Otwin up by his neck with one hand. "At long last, Father's vengeance is complete. And *your* father's cruelty repaid in full." Now he brought his other hand up, closed it around the king's throat, and shoved him against the wall.

The king beat against Wudga's arms.

He might as well have tried to wrestle a mammoth. Wudga's muscles bulged as he squeezed. The king's futile efforts grew slower.

And finally, Wudga dropped the body on the floor.

HERVOR CLENCHED her jaw as Starkad stitched the wound on her arm. Other than the fatigue of battle and the slight wooziness of blood loss, she didn't feel ill.

"So it's not poisoned?"

Starkad glanced at her face for the barest instant. They sat together in the king's chamber while Ewald and Wudga looted the castle. No more guards challenged them. Maybe it was that Wudga now bore Mimung and claimed descent from Princess Bodvild—and was he then truly the son of the dark smith Volund? Or maybe it was that Starkad had killed a score of men single-handedly. Or maybe no one felt over-much loyalty to a dead man who clearly would not pay them any longer.

Regardless, those Njararan warriors who had not fled had joined in the looting.

Finally, Starkad shook his head. "I have heard no tales of such, and many stories do speak of the fell, cursed blade wielded by the king of Njarar. You'll live." He rose then, mumbling something under his breath.

Hervor prodded the wound on her arm. Not poisoned maybe, but it hurt like Hel herself had spit on it. "I ... I really thought I was going to die."

"Well, you fucking could have! I never should have agreed to bring you along."

"What the fuck is that supposed to mean?"

Starkad waved a dismissive hand in her direction. "It means naught, Hervor. Not a damned thing."

She lurched to her feet. Then she shoved him. "No. No, you say what you fucking want to say. We might have all died this night. So tell me, great Starkad, what is it you need to say? Huh? Is this about me being a woman again?"

His face faltered a moment.

Oh. It *was* about that shit again. "Fuck you, Starkad."

He opened his mouth, then shut it, shaking his head.

"No you don't!" She shoved him again, pushed him hard enough he stumbled against the wall. "You don't get to walk away. I fought by your side on Thule, and I fought by your side tonight. I have earned your godsdamned respect a half dozen times over!"

"I ... suppose you have."

"Damn right. We were *glorious* tonight. Odin himself must have watched our victory."

The man winced. He fucking winced.

"What *is* it with you?" She got right up in his face. She was damned tired of this. "Are you afraid of women? Why? Does your cock not work right? Got a little limp wad of shame stuck between your legs?"

Now he pushed her back so hard she stumbled and fell on her arse. "It works fine."

"Prove it!" The words left her mouth before she realized she even intended to say them. Huh. So that was said. Her pulse was pounding through her neck, pumping so hard her whole body felt like it would tremble apart. She knew blood still plastered her face, her hair. Not exactly some beautiful princess. But whatever. She'd fucking said it. No backing down now. "Fucking prove it!"

Starkad's hands twitched, his face an unreadable mix of emotions.

She jerked at the laces of her trousers, yanking the damned things away as fast as she could. "If you're not afraid of what I've got between *my* legs then you get over here and—"

Before she could even finish the sentence he had seized her and flung her up on the king's bed. Starkad tore away her trousers but only managed to get one leg of them off her, the other tangled around her boot. And then his own pants were about his ankles.

And his cock punched inside her.

Drew a gasp from her.

He pounded into her like a smith at an anvil. Hervor wrapped her legs around his waist, her arms around his neck. Bit his ear until he cried out in pain. She rolled atop him and worked with equal fervor. Until he flung her down and mounted her again.

"Do it!" she half shouted, half moaned at him. "Prove to me ... that you ..."

He pinned her arms down and almost snarled at her. Her chest was heaving. Her whole body arched and convulsed without further thought on her part. And Starkad gasped, finally slumping down to lay atop her.

Panting, Hervor rolled him off from her.

She lay very still.

It had been amazing.

And she had no idea how to feel about that.

6

*E*ven with the sun up, the Njarar castle felt chill, almost hostile. Like some noxious force from the Otherworlds brushed against this place. Perhaps that was not so very far from the truth. The dvergar had wrought this place, and Starkad had always heard of their cruelty. Matched, perhaps, by old Nidud and his heir.

And by Volund and *his* heir?

So then, had these halls seen such darkness that they had become stained with it, saturated with suffering and hatred that would not die? Starkad walked alongside Wudga, and the man took in this place. Many of the former soldiers of Otwin had sworn themselves to Wudga—when he had promised them riches drawn from the king's hoard. Others began looting themselves, convinced they could get away with it.

Or perhaps the treasures here were as cursed as the runeblades themselves, as all else wrought by dvergar.

And if dark deeds could indeed infect a place like a rot that would never heal, then it must eventually be the fate of all Midgard to drown in such darkness. For everywhere

Starkad had ever wandered, he'd found war and murder and worse things.

He pressed his palms against his eyes.

"Something vexes you?" Wudga asked. The man seemed changed, almost pale ... exhaustion from the battle?

Starkad shook his head. A great many things, perhaps, but none he truly wished to discuss, least of all with this man. Fucking Hervor was like to prove a mistake. He'd left her, asleep on the king's bed, and come to wander these halls as if he might for even a moment forget what he'd just done. How much he'd fucking enjoyed it.

Had he wanted to do that with her already? Had he been fooling himself?

And, damn it, how had she made him so introspective this day? His musings on the rotting of Midgard were even more pointless than worrying over the nature of his relationship with that woman. It all amounted to naught.

Starkad cleared his throat. "I simply find myself pondering where to go next."

"Have you not pledged your services to the woman?" Wudga snickered. "Actually, it sounded like you already served her well, but perhaps not the service you promised her."

Right. Of course half the castle would have heard that. Neither Hervor nor himself had made much effort at subtlety or quiet. And even thinking about it, he felt himself start to rise again. Maybe he ought to see her and ... oh. Hel. Where did he let his mind wander now?

Wudga led him down a staircase that descended deep into the mountain. A hidden treasure vault?

The man glanced back at Starkad. "The dvergar called such places deep forges. Here, Nidud imprisoned my father in darkness and forced him to craft all manner of wonders."

Or horrors, depending on one's perspective. And now even Wudga carried a runeblade. The very treasure Starkad so fervently sought lay slung over the back of a man not five feet away. A simple shove off the staircase and Wudga would plummet into darkness. Starkad grit his teeth against such unworthy thoughts. Except ... this mission would have failed without him. Was he not owed his due?

But Wudga had promised him silver and appeared intent to pay that. He had always said the runeblade was his own prize. Starkad clenched his fists at his side lest they try to draw his blades on their own. He could not trust himself. Not since the curse. Maybe not even before that ...

Much as he wanted to blame all his crimes, all his failings upon the Otherworldly ... something rotten lay within Starkad's breast. Always had.

They descended deep beneath the ground, the fragile flicker of Wudga's torch disappearing into the vast recesses of the cavern that spread out around them. Eventually, the stairs deposited them on a landing that led to a stone bridge spanning an ill-looking lake. Starkad frowned, staring at the too-still waters.

Wudga's torch dimmed as though he hooded a lantern, and Starkad jerked up, hand on his sword hilt.

"Peace," Wudga said. "He is coming."

"Who is—"

A slight shuffle answered him, as a man limped closer. He remained just out of the radius of the torchlight, as if he feared it. Or rather it failed to cast illumination onto him, as if the light feared *him*. Like living shadows, and the hints of gray skin and jet-black hair. A fell creature whose presence set Starkad's soul stirring, demanding he flee this place and retreat into daylight. The shadows seemed to whisper in some forgotten, hissing tongue, filled with loathing of all life.

"You have done well, my son."

Yes. For this was Volund himself. The dark smith whose vengeance upon Nidud had become legend. Vengeance, which Wudga had finally completed for his father.

Wudga dropped to one knee, unslung Mimung, and offered it to Volund with both hands.

The smith chuckled, the sound of it like nails churning Starkad's brain. "That is for you to bear and earn your fame as you see best. It will serve you well."

Wudga rose, shouldering the blade in a single motion. "Yes, Father."

Volund looked past his son. At Starkad. His gaze made Starkad's skin crawl. "And you. Champion of Odin, off collecting the lost runeblades."

"I'm not ..." Not what? Hunting the runeblades? Was he not just thinking how badly he needed one? But he didn't do it for Odin. At least ... Starkad hoped he wasn't doing it all for Odin. He could no longer trust his own mind, his own heart. His own dreams. Was he so naive as to think Odin did not use him? The Ás used all men.

"Are you not, then?" The shadows seemed to fold among themselves such that Starkad imagined Volund shrugging. "Perhaps then you do not wish to hear of the lost treasures of Glaesisvellir? Of the runeblade Skofnung? Or the others ..."

The very words were like a blow to the gut. An irresistible, unstoppable urge that seized his chest and took control of his throat. Spoke his words for him. "There is a runeblade in Glaesisvellir?"

"Oh ... yes ... lost, long ago, when the Old Kingdoms fell. And fell so deeply. Taken there, and perhaps, even beyond."

Starkad took a step toward the darkness that was Volund and yet saw the man—the creature—no more clearly than before. "Where is Glaesisvellir?"

"Why ... beyond the Midgard Wall, of course."

Starkad stared dumbly into the darkness. In ... Utgard? Starkad liked to push all limits, but he had not yet ventured beyond the wall. "I ... you're working with Odin."

The darkness merely chuckled at that, once again seeming to tear through Starkad's mind.

And then the presence slowly abated, the torch returning to its full illumination, scant though it was.

"So," Wudga said. "You will venture to Jotunheim?"

"I have no choice. If that is where the runeblade lies, there I go."

Wudga nodded. "I will see you well stocked with silver and provisions for such a trek."

At that he inclined his head. Such was only his due, after all. Before he could set out for Jotunheim, though, he had made an oath to Hervor. He would not break it, whatever mistakes might have gone between them.

"So," Wudga said. "I have heard of tales of Glaesisvellir, stories carried on the wind about the land and its famed King Godmund."

"A jotunn?"

"Indeed."

Starkad grimaced. His dealings with jotunnar had been ill, thus far.

"Though the king is not the darkest tale spreading out from Glaesisvellir."

"Meaning?"

"Whispers ... that the Veil grows thin. That the worlds bleed together and all you think you know means less than naught."

The Veil ... that was what völvur called the barrier separating Midgard from whatever lay beyond. "Thin? Thinner than this place?"

Wudga chuckled, the sound marginally less unnerving than it had been coming from his father. Indeed, Wudga seemed a great deal like his father these days. "Oh. Yes. Much ... or so the tales say." The man smirked. "You cannot find the place, though."

"Why not?"

"Will you wander the frozen wastes for all eternity? Without the Sight, you cannot hope to navigate the vast wilds beyond the wall."

And how did Wudga know so much of what went on beyond the Midgard Wall? Had he learned this from his father? "So tell me where to go."

"Does Odin not haunt your dreams, warrior? Have you not asked yourself why he can reach you? Perhaps you have a latent gift for the Sight and require but the means to harness it."

Oh.

Intriguing ... and horrifying, in its own right. Was Starkad to be like those fell seers and völvur, driven apart from mankind but unearthly visions? But then, Starkad was already quite apart from most of society. "How?"

"There is a fluid, lingering in toxic pools, still enduring from when this world was young. A poison, perhaps, but one some claim gave rise to life."

What the fuck was he on about now? Starkad leaned back against the wall. His patience with Volund and his son was starting to wear thin. "Speak plainly."

"This ... fluid, the eitr, flows through the veins of linnorms."

"Even if I knew where to find a dragon, I have little inclination to fight one." Though the glory of such ... no. It was mist-madness. No man survived contact with such ancient beasts. Not even Starkad.

"You need not. One might also find some fleeting streams of eitr in the deep places. As might be found not so far from here, in caverns once home to dvergar. I can tell you where ... if you are willing to delve deeply."

Another dverg treasure hoard? Oh, Starkad would delve deep indeed for such wonders, to say naught of this eitr.

"But you say it is poison?"

"Yes ... I can brew it into a draught that may serve your purpose ... but aught worth doing has risks, yes?"

Oh, indeed. And Starkad would take such risks gladly.

So then, let them make haste to fulfill his oath to Hervor. And when that was done, Starkad had darker treks to begin. For Wudga must surely speak the truth ... Odin's interest in Starkad had come from long winters back.

And that meant, like Wudga, Starkad might well have a touch of the Otherworldly about him ...

7

Twenty-Three Years Ago

TWO WINTERS since Tyr had brought Starkad and Vikar along to Andalus, to fight against the Serklanders, and Starkad had won his share of glory in a half dozen battles in that time. The foreign empire did not oft try its luck at the crossing of late, and that left a lot of long days, longer nights. Boredom.

Lots of time to train.

Starkad grinned at Ganelon as the paladin panted, pacing around him.

They'd all called Starkad mist-mad for trying to wield two full-sized swords at once. Oh, but Tyr had insisted both brothers learn to fight left-handed—the man had taught himself to do so after losing his right hand to the beast that had killed their mother. They had done so, sure enough. And then Starkad had thought, if he could fight with either hand ... why not both?

Tyr had thrashed him the first time they had sparred like that. Roland had done so, too. All the paladins he'd challenged. Even Vikar. And the men laughed.

No one was laughing now.

He'd fought three men at once, and all now sat on their arses, nursing welts and scrapes and bruised pride.

Ganelon, too, his chest heaved, gaze locked on Starkad's slowly twirling blades.

Every day, every night of their interminable exile here, Starkad had practiced swinging these.

Tyr had not been fast enough to stop Fenrir from tearing out Mother's throat. But Starkad was getting faster. And the fastest man was the only one who mattered.

Ganelon charged in again, a mighty swing. It was probably fast, but it seemed lethargic to Starkad, every movement exaggerated and projected ahead of time. With one blade, Starkad knocked aside Ganelon's sword. The other, he slapped against the paladin's gut, doubling him over. An instant later, he brought the first blade round, slapped the flat against Ganelon's arse, and sent him sprawling.

"Boy moves like lightning," Ganelon grumbled to no one in particular, as far as Starkad could tell.

Starkad chuckled, thrust his swords into the sand, and offered the man a hand up. In truth, when he'd first arrived, Ganelon had been the one to help Starkad learn advanced techniques with the blade. Roland's paladins—as he called them—proved some of the greatest fighters in the South Realms. Many of the Aesir dismissed that as irrelevant, thought their southern allies weak and small.

Starkad saw something more in them, though. Lacking North Realmer brawn, they made up for it with speed and precision. The fastest man was the only one who mattered. And so Starkad had trained under Tyr, learning to fight left-handed. He'd trained with Ganelon and mastered efficiency of motion. He'd practiced archery with Astolfo, and he'd pushed himself on long-distance runs and tracking with Hermod.

In the end, there would be no one faster, no one better. And Starkad would ensure what happened to Mother ... did not ever again happen to those he loved.

That was his oath to himself.

Starkad motioned for his next contender to wait while he snatched up a skin of water and drank deep. He eyed the others waiting, so many men all eager to challenge him. Shieldmaidens, too, and he'd fought some few of them. Managed to get no few of them to tumble into his bed afterward as well.

Yes, Starkad rather liked women.

Shame these southerners didn't seem to bring their women along to battle. Starkad would not have minded having the chance to stick it in a soft southern woman and see if there was a difference.

A commotion began in the south of the camp. Shouting, a crowd gathering. Were the Serks trying the Straits again? No ... no sound of weapons beating on shields, no drums of war.

Starkad glanced at Ganelon who scowled, then together they made their way over to the gathered crowd.

In the midst of the throng, Tyr stood across from Roland, his clipped, angry words not quite carrying over the grumbling of the crowd. Roland seemed even more engaged. The Vallander commander spent a great deal of time with Starkad's ... father. Acknowledging that left a bitter taste in Starkad's mouth. Tyr had killed the man Starkad had called father. But the man had then sworn an oath that he was Starkad's—though not Vikar's—true sire. And Mother had loved him first, Starkad knew that much.

Behind Roland, Starkad saw him. Vikar, beaten. Chained.

What the fuck was this?

Starkad pushed men aside to get to his brother. Punched a man who tried to bar his way and sent another sprawling with a heavy shove. "Explain this!"

Tyr and Roland both turned to him now. Tyr's face worn, maybe even resigned. Roland's eyes lit with a fury Starkad did not remember seeing in him before.

"Your brother disobeyed my orders," the Vallander said.

"I killed the godsdamned enemy!" Vikar shouted, then spat. "Is that not why we are here?"

Tyr stepped around Roland to cuff Vikar. "Be silent, boy."

Starkad's fingers itched to thrash them both. "You beat and chained him ... for killing Serks?" It was hard to keep his voice level, to keep from shouting. To keep from killing.

"No," Roland said. "He was apprehended for disobeying my orders—and endangering his fighting brothers in so doing. Men died rescuing him from an ill-advised charge against an enemy already in retreat."

"You were going to let them escape to come at us again—"

Tyr cuffed him a second time.

Starkad's hand closed around his sword hilt, not even realizing he had reached for it. "Release. My. Brother."

"Starkad," Tyr snapped. "I am handling this. Find somewhere else to be."

"Release Vikar, *now*."

Roland took a step forward, his glare almost enough to

make Starkad falter. Almost. "Son. You seem to forget which of us gives the orders in this camp. I command our forces. And now I'm commanding you to listen to your father and walk away."

Starkad spat. He drew his sword ... he tried.

Ganelon's fist caught him in the gut. It blew all the wind from Starkad's lungs. Before he could even rise, rough hands seized him, jerked him up, and stole his blades from their scabbards.

Florismart, another paladin, stalked over.

"Starkad!" Tyr bellowed.

Florismart's fist connected with Starkad's jaw. His world spun, his legs losing all strength.

Everything went hazy.

STARKAD TOSSED ASIDE the rags he'd used to staunch the blood from his nose. He sat in Tyr's tent, still slightly dazed. Vikar was there—unchained, finally—and Tyr himself. Hanging his head. Defeated. The so-called champion of the Aesir, the legendary warrior, looking broken. Useless.

A slave came in bearing mead, which Tyr drank, then motioned to be taken to Vikar. Finally, Starkad got his turn.

"So?" he asked, wiping his mouth after drinking deeply.

"A Vallander who so disobeyed his commander would find himself strung up," Tyr said. "Nor can I well ignore Vikar's actions. In pursuit of his own glory, he endangered our oath-sworn allies. But I can't see him hung either."

Starkad nodded. "Then where do we go?"

"There is only one punishment befitting his crimes, an Ás punishment. He must go where the wind takes him, welcome no longer in Valland ... nor Asgard."

"Banished?" Vikar blurted. "You cannot be fucking serious. All I did was kill some Hel-cursed Serklanders!"

From the sound of it, Vikar had done a bit more. Tyr spoke the truth, little though Starkad loved it. Exile was the traditional punishment for betrayal. But then again ... fuck tradition.

"What authority does Roland have over Asgard? Send us back. Vikar may have earned the wrath of the southerners, but he may also have earned an apple of Yggdrasil."

Tyr scoffed. "You think the boy deserves a reward? The ultimate reward? Boy shamed us. Shamed all the Aesir." The man cracked his neck. Groaned. "No. Banishment it is. Odin was nearby, though. Came to speak to me over it. He's made allies in Sviarland, allies who might have use for Vikar. Give him a chance at a glorious life."

Vikar sputtered. "But ... the apples?"

"Those are for Aesir, son. I am left with no choice but to strip you of that title."

"And me." The words were bitter in Starkad's mouth.

"What?" Vikar said.

Tyr spun on him. "Son, you have no idea what—"

"Do not call me *son*, Tyr. Were I your son, you would have fought for my brother. If you cast him out, I go with him."

Tyr glowered now. "Your bravado and threats change naught, Starkad. Urd is cruel. You might yet claim the prize of an apple ... if you don't do this."

Starkad sneered at his would-be father. "If my brother is no Ás, neither am I."

Grumbling about fool children, Tyr rose, shook his head. And ducked out of the tent.

Fuck. Fuck them all.

Starkad turned to Vikar. "Gather supplies. We leave camp at first light."

"You did not have to come with me."

"Of course I did." Starkad stalked outside. The others were watching him. Maybe just that they'd heard about Vikar. Or maybe word had already spread that he too was leaving them. Well, Hel take every last one of them. All this war, all this training, fighting. It ought to have earned both brothers an apple of Yggdrasil. Earned them the right to live forever, to fight forever, to reign in glory over the world.

Instead, they left here with even less than they'd come. Without a people to call their own.

A pair of shieldmaidens sat at a fire, chatting. Good then. Best get one last romp before he abandoned the Aesir forever.

But as he approached, the women looked at one another, rose and slipped away.

That was new.

Starkad frowned.

Shook his head.

Well, there would be women wherever he next trod.

As he passed through the camp, an old man in a wide-brimmed hat stepped into his path. No vagrant belonged in a war camp, and this man had seen too many winters to be a soldier ... so ...

"King Odin?"

The old man nodded, then motioned for Starkad to follow. That drew a frown. He didn't look like Odin—not that Starkad had seen the king too oft—but somehow, he'd known it must be him. War must have honed his instincts.

The old man led him away from camp, into dark woods.

"You are vexed at being denied an apple," Odin said without bothering to turn around. Shadows drenched the king of Asgard, hiding even his disguise. Even knowing the Aesir had once been men, Starkad could barely stop from balking at Odin's presence. At his ... airs of mystery. At his touch of the Otherworlds.

Starkad grit his teeth. If he was no longer Ás himself, Odin was no longer his king. And he owed the man no further respect. "Would not you be vexed, having fought harder than any other for a prize and to have it snatched away?"

Odin turned slowly. "Harder than any other? Are you so certain no other man has suffered and fought as you have ... ah, well it matters naught, Starkad. You have but to abandon your brother and come into my service, and all you desire may yet come to you."

"Abandon my brother?" Starkad snorted. "Would you abandon yours? I think not." He resisted the urge to spit— barely. He might not have owed Odin respect, but only a fool would antagonize a man ... being ... of such power.

"I cannot allow an apple to fall to those who will not serve the will of Asgard."

No. Starkad supposed that only a fool would willingly give away such a gift, especially when too few of the treasures remained for his own loyal servants. So the only answer he could offer was to shrug.

"And yet ... you may yet serve and earn a reward. Go to King Gylfi in Sviarland and serve him well, and you may serve me in so doing."

Win Odin's favor ... no. Starkad shook his head. "I serve no man, for I have no people left. And I will make my own way, King of the Aesir."

"Urd is cruel, Starkad. We will see each other again in the days to come ... in the darkest of nights."

Starkad shook his head and left the old man in the

forest. He was done with such things, forever. Done being one more tool in Odin's arsenal.

Starkad's life, his urd, they would be his own to make.

8

Ostergotland lay south of Njarar, several days' walk in the best of weather. With winter settling, Hervor and Starkad had already travelled for three days and were not even halfway there. The snows had not settled enough for dog sleds, so walking appeared the only option. Shame.

Most of those long hours, he barely spoke to her.

Hervor cleared her throat to try again as they passed under the deeper reaches of Deeppine. "There are bogs all over ... best be wary."

"I walked these lands many times. Even before you were born."

Right. Fine. "So how old are you, then? I've heard tales that you don't age so much like a normal man."

Starkad cast a glance over at her, his face unreadable but certainly not warm. Badgering him into sleeping with her had clearly not been her best idea. Then again, Hervor had a lot of poor ideas in retrospect. "After this job is done, I'll be moving on."

"What? Where?"

"Farther than you would care to travel, I am certain, and no place you'd have heard of."

"Huh." She spat to the side of the path. "Good to see your arrogance is back. I was starting to worry over your health. Seems maybe someone needs another reminder—I fought that draug prince on Thule. As far as I know, that's not even really part of Midgard."

"Nor is the kingdom where I soon walk."

"Wait, what?"

Starkad paused then, and Hervor drew up short, turning back to look at him. "Hervor ... I must seek another dverg ruin. And should I find that ... I go next to Glaesisvellir in Jotunheim. Tales speak of great treasures."

"And you didn't have your fill of treasure hunting in Thule?"

Did his so-called curse truly compel him to such recklessness? Or was that merely an excuse to not take responsibility for his own failings?

Starkad shrugged and started walking again. "What did we come away with, truly? A few silver coins, a few gems. A runeblade taken by Ecgtheow?"

"The runeblade ..." Was that what this was about? "You regret giving it to him. Or ... are you angry that *I* gave it to him?"

He scoffed, not bothering to look at her. Which was not an answer.

Hervor scowled as she followed him down the path. Had they not promised the blade to Tiny—to Ecgtheow? What had he expected her to do? Break her oath? She'd never do that ... nor, had she thought, would Starkad. Why could the damned man never figure out what he really wanted?

"It will be hard going," he said a few moments later. "Assaulting Upsal in winter, I mean."

So he wanted to change the subject. Fine. She had recruited him for a reason, and it was past time she got back to it. Sometimes she wanted to like this man, true, wanted to think him a friend. Odin alone knew what Starkad actually thought. But none of that mattered. Hervor had her own oath, one to bring down the Ynglings. And that meant taking on Upsal. That meant Starkad leading Haki's champions.

"King Haki has a fleet of longships. We'll descend on our foes before they know what's coming for them."

"Sailing the Gandvik in winter poses its own risks. The storms can crop up with little warning and leave us all prey to Rán."

Hervor had spent enough time on a ship to know that fear. "We'll hug the coast. No one will be meeting the mermaid queen this winter. None of ours, at least. Trust me, Starkad, this will be fast and brutal. Then you can go and do whatever you want—even throw your life away in Jotunheim."

Starkad glanced up at the sky, though he could not have possibly made out much through the canopy and the mist. "I think it will be dark before long. Perhaps we should see about finding a camp."

Another night in the woods with little conversation between them. How appealing. "If we press, I think we can reach my grandfather's hall in an hour."

"Your grandfather?"

"Jarl Bjalmar is sworn to King Haki."

Starkad grunted and rubbed his scraggly beard. "Lead on then."

59

MATT LARKIN

Darkness had settled before they reached the town, and the gates were closed. She could almost feel it as archers drew a bead on her when she approached.

"I am no vaettr!" she called up to them.

"You're out in the mist at night."

She took another step closer, slowly. Alarm these bastards and they'd shoot her before they had the first clue who she was. That didn't sound the least bit pleasant. "It's Hervor—Bjalmar's granddaughter."

Murmuring above. Men shifting.

A warrior leaned over the wall just a bit, waving a torch out to his side. "Step into the light."

She did so.

"It's her," the man said a moment later.

A pair of warriors escorted her to the main hall—where Gunther was waiting. The thegn looked even older than when she'd last seen him. Like one who had no more business wielding a sword, though he'd taught her well enough with one in days long gone.

"So you're back." He looked to Starkad. "And this is?"

"Starkad Eightarms."

Gunther recoiled, then visibly stifled his shock and offered Hervor's friend a respectful nod. "Well then, I'll take you to see the jarl."

"I don't believe you ever mentioned being nobility," Starkad whispered as he strode beside her to the back of the hall.

No. She had not. Nor was she quite certain why she'd let him learn so much about her now. Except ... Odin's balls. What was she doing with him, anyway? Starkad was even more fucked up than her. He couldn't have stayed in one place if his life depended on it. No, now normal adventures were not enough. Now he had to go delving

60

beyond all mortal ken into places touched by the Otherworld.

Imbecile.

Gunther plodded over to Hervor's grandfather's side and whispered in his ear.

Strange that her mother was not here to greet her. It was too early for her to have retired for the night.

"Hervor," Grandfather said and rose. "It is good you have returned."

"Only for the night. We need supplies for a short journey. At dawn we must continue on toward Haki's hall."

Grandfather glanced at Gunther as if the thegn ought to have had any say whatsoever in this hall. "Hervor ... walk with me. Gunther ... see to our guest."

Gunther nodded, then motioned for Starkad to follow him to a table.

Actually, hot food and some mead were about all Hervor wanted now herself, but she allowed Grandfather to guide her into his private chamber behind the main hall. He motioned to a chair, and she sat, her stomach suddenly roiling, though not with any thought of food.

"What's going on?"

He sighed as he collapsed into a chair across from her, then let his forehead fall to his palm. For the barest instant, his shoulders bobbed and when he looked up, he was blinking away a tear. How unmanly. And unlike Grandfather. What the fuck?

And then it hit her.

For there was only one thing that might cause him to react thus.

"Where ... is my ... *mother*?"

"She ... fell ill."

"In the summer?" Hervor lurched to her feet. It

happened from time to time, but summer was supposed to be safe. "I must see her." As if she did not know. As if she did not ... did not ... already understand ...

His face ... "She's gone, Hervor."

"Y-you didn't even send for me?"

He sighed, shaking. "We ... tried. Sent men to the king, but he said you'd gone north. And so we had to send her on her way."

She clenched her jaw and leaned down on the armrests of his chair. "You mean you already fucking burned her. You burned her without me! Without her *daughter!*"

He leapt to his feet, sending her stumbling backward. Raised his hand like he might slap her. "Losing one's parents is inevitable, Hervor. I, however, have lost *my* daughter. And you *dare* to raise your voice to me as if I have wronged you? I have suffered my grief alone while you gallivanted around with that mercenary monster you brought into my house!"

What? Grandfather rarely showed overmuch temper. When he did ... Hervor fell back another step, still uncertain if he planned to hit her. Or whether she would defend herself if he tried. "You mean Starkad?"

"I can think of few men in all Sviarland with so ill a reputation."

"I was sent to recruit him by our *king.*"

Grandfather waved that away, then glanced about the room as if wanting something to steady himself on. "Listen to me, girl. I have indulged your whims as best I could, let you train as a shieldmaiden, and find service to the king. But now your mother is gone, and I am not like to see many more winters. Our land needs a ruler. It is past time for you to give over your foolery, find a husband, and pop out an heir or three."

Hervor sputtered, not even able to form a response to

that. Did he seriously expect her to give over her oath to her father, to her kin? "I have a mission to complete."

"King Haki got on well enough for many years without Hervor at his side, and I dare say he'll manage to live on without you."

"I'm not only talking about my oath to the king, though now you mention it—"

"Enough! You returned from Thule a scarred, bitter wreck and from all I can tell, barely alive at all. You tempt your urd with your petty quest to avenge those who neither want nor need your aid. Your father and all his kin are long gone from this world. Their side of the family is not the only one to which you have a duty! Or perhaps you would like to see us too restless and wakeful after death?"

Hervor spat on his floor. "Were I to speak to the king of your words ..."

"So you would now betray your family again?"

No. She would not do that, whatever she might threaten. She had done enough damage in her days with Red-Eye's Boys. Nor, however, was she going to stand here and let the man browbeat her into marrying some arrogant jarl's son while her oath lay unfulfilled.

"Give us the supplies or do not, Grandfather. Either way, we leave at first light and go to join Haki. And when he claims the throne of Upsal, I will be there at his side. And he will think you a good and loyal supporter to have sent him so great an ally."

She spun and left, unwilling to let him get in another word.

PART II

Fourth Moon
Year 28, Age of the Aesir

9

Screams rang out through Fyris Woods, as men died slowly and quickly. Hundreds of corpses clogged the paths, blanketed the roots, made navigating treacherous. Blood and guts and shit coated the trees and Hervor as well.

Panting and reeling, she dodged around another tree.

An arrow thunked into the wood beside her, and she stumbled and scrambled back the way she'd come. So much chaos. Couldn't think ... couldn't tell what direction that missile had come from.

Hard to even say who was on which side.

A man bellowed, charged her with an axe over his head. A swift thrust from Tyrfing. The blade punched through his chest and stole all strength from his intended blow. Hervor kicked him, shoving the body away.

They had attacked with surprise, slaughtered so many of Ochilaik's men. But now everything had gone to shit.

Shit and blood, like the damned trees.

It was impossible to hold any kind of line in the forest.

Hervor had meant to stick by Haki's side at first, but Ochilaik's thegns had led a counterattack.

Leaning against a tree, she wiped blood from her mouth with the back of her hand. She'd seen a lot of battles, but war on this scale ... it was something else.

Two armies clashing in the woods.

And naught but death everywhere she turned.

So be it then, she had brought death here. Death, with a golden pommel, always hungry for more blood. And she would feed it until she found Ochilaik. She'd kill the bastard herself and not only fulfill her oath but win high praise from Haki.

A few more deep breaths to steady herself and she raced back out, ducking between more trees. There, a cluster of men all fighting.

One spun about several others, wielding two swords and engaging at least five men. Some of Ochilaik's own thegns and champions ... fighting Starkad. If he was there, the king of Upsal must be close.

Belting out her own war cry, she charged back into the fray. Tyrfing darted around shields and under guards, drawing fatal scratches along the necks and sides and limbs of a half dozen warriors who did not know death had already claimed them. No mail could turn aside the runeblade. No armor could protect against such a weapon.

From the look of things, Ochilaik must have lost damn nigh to half his army.

There, Haki's brother Hagbard swung a maul at a big man bearing a battleaxe and shield. Ochilaik's man leapt sideways out of the path of the mighty blow, the hammer smacking into the ground. His own counter caught Hagbard on the shoulder. Only the prince's mail saved him, and still the blow sent him reeling, weaponless. Arm hanging limp.

Damn it.

That must be one of Ochilaik's champions. Geigad or Svipdag?

Hervor slew another warrior, then raced in, intercepting the champion before he could close in and finish off Hagbard.

"I am Hervard, thegn to Haki! Face me."

Up close, the man seemed even larger. Six and half feet, maybe more. He spit and sneered. "Geigad Rockfist." The big man eyed Tyrfing. "I know what that is, boy. And I think I shall make an even greater name for myself with it ... after I ram it so far up your arse it scrapes your teeth."

Colorful. Under other circumstances, Hervor might have traded insults with him. But she wasn't going to intimidate this man. And that meant naught remained left to be said. Geigad stood between her and vengeance against Ochilaik.

Hervor raised her shield up between them, Tyrfing held ready just off to her side.

Geigad beat his axe against his shield once, hard. Even as the motion finished, he sprang at her, much faster than his big form ought to have allowed. His axe came down so quickly Hervor only just managed to get her shield in position. The axe clanged against it, chipped the wood. Numbed her arm. Again and once again Geigad rained blows upon her shield. After the third, her arm wasn't working.

She jerked Tyrfing up in a clumsy counter, but he batted it away with his own shield. She was too far out of position. She had to get around—

Geigad snapped his own shield into hers with such force the impact lifted her off her feet. Without balance, she flailed in the air for a bare instant before crashing down into the bloody muck. Tyrfing slipped from her fingers, though she clenched her shield even tighter.

The big man was on her in a heartbeat. Another axe blow on her shield. Another.

Hagbard thrust a spear at him, and Geigad twisted, knocking it away on his shield. The reprieve gave Hervor enough time to snatch up Tyrfing and scramble to her feet. Couldn't catch her breath.

Everything hurt.

Arm wouldn't respond right.

Couldn't feel the fingers in her shield hand.

Damn thing was splintered all to pieces too. A few more blows and it would crumble like kindling.

Hervor lunged at Geigad again, swiped with Tyrfing. With one arm limp, every blow felt off-center, every strike sloppy. She couldn't properly get her weight behind a swing. But all it should take was a scratch and at least she'd take this big fuck down with her.

Moving too fast once again, he knocked away Tyrfing with his axe while smashing his shield into Hagbard's face. The king's brother crumpled like a discarded shirt.

Geigad spat. Turned on her. "You and me, boy."

Grunting with the pain, she pulled her shield back into position. And he kept advancing.

She was going to die.

The realization was sudden, certain.

She had Tyrfing, but Geigad was bigger, stronger, faster. Had more reach. He was ... just plain better. A champion feared throughout all the North Realms. Only a few men like that alive. She'd killed one, once, in Orvar-Oddr.

Killed him—through treachery. Stabbed him when he was exhausted and had no idea she intended it.

She was, after all, a treacherous bitch. About to get what she deserved.

"Starkad ..." she tried to shout the name, though it came

wheezy, winded as she was. She backed away, not nigh to fast enough to escape anyone, much less this killer.

Geigad sneered. "Meet your death with honor, boy. Maybe Odin will take you to Valhalla."

Maybe. Or after all the wretchedness she had wrought, maybe Hel herself would come to claim Hervor's soul ...

"This is ... Tyrfing ..." She hefted the sword. "It will have your blood."

The champion smiled grimly and charged. She raised her shield to block—and he slammed his into it once again, this time driving her almost straight into the ground. She swept up Tyrfing to chop out his knees. His axe came down faster.

It smashed into her clavicle and ribs. Fire erupted inside her as bones broke. The axe tore into flesh and muscle, even through her mail. Hervor gurgled on the pain, choked on her own scream. Collapsed, even as Tyrfing clipped the man's calf and fell from her useless sword arm.

Geigad faltered, staring at where the sword had grazed him.

Through the blinding haze of pain, through the blood and muck splattered over her eyes, still she saw. The look on his face.

He knew he was as dead as she was.

Bastard.

10

*I*t happened fast. Geigad's axe descending on Hervor before Starkad even realized how much danger she was in. The way she fell like that. The big man stumbled like she'd cut him, but even if he knew what that meant, he wasn't dead yet. Nor like to live long enough to die of that wound.

Starkad snarled as he dashed toward the pair, swords flashing. Geigad tried to turn on him. One of Starkad's swords snaked in to score a hit on the man's weapon arm. The other slammed down on his shield, then jerked back up. Tore a gouge out of his face.

Geigad reeled.

It was all the opening Starkad needed. His other blade snapped up in a tight arc that opened Geigad's throat.

Starkad started to turn to Hervor when Svipdag the Mad charged in. Starkad had seen the man fight before, always a sword and axe pair, aggression over a shield. Not unlike Starkad. Fast and brutal.

But Starkad would be faster. The fastest man was the only one who mattered.

Round and round they spun.

Parry, dodge. Riposte.

Parry.

Starkad grunted and whipped his blades in rapidly changing arcs, trying to catch his foe off guard. But Svipdag, Scourge of Lappmarken, had no doubt seen Starkad fight as well. Every move countered. Every advantage—negated.

More than aught else in the world, Starkad wanted to glance over at Hervor. To see if she lived. To *know* she did.

But he dared not take his eyes off Svipdag for even a moment. Here he had managed to find an actual challenge for his skills, the likes of which he had rarely found among mortal foes. Svipdag's own uncanny speed allowed him to dodge blows that would have decapitated most men.

Svipdag swept low with the axe, forced Starkad to leap backward, then twist out of the way of a sudden follow-up with the sword. Starkad knocked the blade aside, countered with his other, and fell back when Svipdag parried that as well.

His foe backed away a moment, panting. Not that Starkad was opposed to the chance to catch his own breath.

Now he did cast the briefest of glances at Hervor. The shieldmaiden had begun to crawl along the ground. Alive for the moment, thank any gods who were listening. But with such a wound ... she did not seem like to stay that way.

"You should be fighting by our side, Eightarms," Svipdag said. "Does your loyalty not lie with the Ynglings?"

"My loyalties lie with individuals, not whole families— much less those who turn on their own kin."

The Lappmarken man scoffed. "Your loyalty lies to silver, same as any mercenary. Same as me."

"Then we have naught else to discuss, do we?"

Svipdag spit, then shook his head, raising that sword high and keeping the axe low.

So then, let them be about it. Starkad roared, charged. High, low. Strikes from every angle, tight and wide. Any chance to slip through the man's defenses. Any chance to get back to ...

Focus!

The woman would get him killed.

His arms ached from swinging the blades so long. His attacks were starting to slow. But then, so were Svipdag's. Starkad threw out another series of strikes, slowing these down on purpose. Svipdag parried each. Again.

Again.

Starkad feinted left and swung with the right.

Svipdag knocked away Starkad's real attack with his axe, ignoring the ploy.

Again Starkad attacked, even slower. Svipdag lunged forward, trying to riposte. This time, Starkad stepped in as well, bringing his second sword up with twice the speed he'd made his other attacks. His blade was too close, lacked strength. It scraped along Svipdag's mail but couldn't cut it. It did, however, cause the other man to lurch over from the impact, probably more out of shock than aught else.

Starkad rammed the pommel of his other blade into Svipdag's chin. Drove him back a few steps. Then he jerked both swords together, the edges tearing out the Mad's throat in a crisscross. Gurgling, the Lappmarken champion dropped to his knees, then pitched over.

Hervor.

Starkad stumbled toward her, his feet threatening to give out from under him.

"Hervor!" His throat seemed hoarse. Worn ragged with his heavy breaths. With battle cries. With sheer exhaustion.

"Hervor!"

Beyond her, Haki had cornered Ochilaik, now without his champion, guarded by a small shield-circle. The Ostergotland king bellowed as he charged the circle, many of his champions behind him. Folke and Kare raced to the fore, guarding their own king.

Starkad tore his eyes away from Haki, to where Hervor lay. She had stopped crawling. Had stopped moving.

He dropped down beside her. Her runeblade lay abandoned, half sunk in mud.

"H-Hervor?"

He rolled her over. Blood plastered all over her mail. It coated it, seeped down into the leathers beneath. The axe blade had chipped the chain links, even broken through in places. The worst of it was the impact, though. It hadn't cut so much, but such a blow ...

Her chest shuddered in another agonized breath.

"Hervor!"

A tremendous cry erupted from within the broken shield circle. There Haki stood, parading around with Ochilaik's head in his hand, held up by the hair. So it was done.

Starkad turned back to Hervor. "Come on. Come on." He looked around. "Someone get a fucking völva here!"

11

Twenty-Two Years Ago

*R*efusing to bow to Odin's whims, Starkad had shunned Sviarland and pressed on, instead to Nidavellir, to Agder, a petty kingdom in the south of the northernmost lands of Midgard. He and Vikar had landed on those shores and come to the court of King Harald, sworn vassal to the dverg King Modsognir.

And the king had welcomed them with open arms, declared them his friends and made them raiders. They had plundered other petty kingdoms in Nidavellir, challenged the forces of Healfdene in Reidgotland, even raided into Sviarland.

And King Harald had grown rich off their efforts, rewarding both brothers in kind. The tribute he had to pay to the dvergar might have ruined a man less inclined to raid or one without such successful allies to carry out those raids. But despite all odds, Agder prospered under Harald. And Starkad knew why.

One arm around Vikar, the other laden with a drinking

horn, Starkad walked Harald's hall. Another raid accomplished, and the brothers' names had begun to spread across the North Realms. One day, they'd be more famous than Tyr.

Starkad liked to think he'd earned it all on his own. Though ... the Ás king did appear in Starkad's dreams on rare occasions. He'd whisper names, places ... sometimes those hints had led to great victories.

Vikar had earned the ear of Harald and would tell the king where to strike next. Despite all Starkad had won for Agder, all the foes he'd slain, Vikar had more way with words.

Now, they had joined the pirate called the Arrow's Point in striking out into Reidgotaland. The man—Orvar-Oddr, he said he was really named—trailed behind, drunk on victory and mead, as Starkad led them all back to Harald's feast hall.

Harald, ever generous, had spared no expense in preparing the tables, now laden with mammoth and whale and shellfish Starkad could not even name. The king himself sat at the head of the table, a grin plastered upon his face, and eyes only slightly bleary with drink. He pounded on the table. "My friends return again!"

"And bearing the greater wealth of Norreyske," Vikar said, then chuckled. "I think Healfdene will be long in recovering from the blow we dealt his thegns."

The king grinned further and slapped the table again. Then he beckoned Vikar and Starkad over. They joined him, Vikar to his right and Starkad to the left. Starkad motioned for a slave to bring a fresh drinking horn, and he drank deeply, savoring the sweet aftertaste.

In the wake of a battle, two things were sweetest. A great draught of mead and plunging deep into a woman's trench. Starkad rather expected to avail himself of both this night.

In fact, he winked at Harald's daughter, Alvilda, though she seemed to only notice Vikar beside her. Damn his fair-tongued brother. Ah, well, there were other women, shield-maidens aplenty, and even slaves who would not object overmuch if he asked one to his chambers.

Harald cleared his throat. Rubbed his nose. "Well, then. I congratulate you all." He raised the horn and his voice both. "And to the Arrow's Point, as well!"

Across the hall, Orvar-Oddr turned to look at the king, nodded, and raised his own horn in salute.

Now the king turned back to Starkad and Vikar. "Ah, well. I would have liked to have gone ... but uh ... I suppose we all know the truth, eh? My days grow few, I think."

"My king," Vikar said.

"Bah! I am not a young man, Vikar, and every man in this hall knows it." He sniffed, then coughed. "Yes. Well, my son is long dead and now I have only Alvilda."

The girl frowned and stared at the table.

Feigned timidity or real? Either way, Starkad found it little appealing however nice her arse and tits.

Harald picked at some mammoth flesh. "When I am gone, Alvilda will need help to rule this kingdom. She'll need a strong man by her side." He looked to Vikar. "And she favors you, my son, though she is not bold enough to speak it."

Indeed, the girl blushed, staring all the harder at the tabletop.

Starkad frowned. It sounded rather like Harald was saying ...

"So then, Vikar. If you would have my daughter, I shall name you my heir. The next king of Agder."

Vikar sputtered a moment, then raised the drinking horn. "It would be my honor."

Harald clapped him on the shoulder. "Then let the wedding feast be arranged!"

At the king's outburst, half the hall turned to look. And seeing their king so pleased, a cheer erupted. Toasts followed and laughter. Skalds poems and wrestling.

And so Vikar's silver tongue would make him a king. Perhaps some things matter more than speed with a sword ... until it came time for battle.

THE WEDDING FEAST was all the greater, more impressive than any Starkad had seen outside of Asgard ... and those days seemed another life now. Events that had happened to someone else. A dream.

And Starkad had woken from that dream long ago.

Drunk and happy, he'd taken a pair of shieldmaidens to bed with him. Sisters, they claimed, though he cared naught one way or the other. He thought them both well pleased, and he laid back, happier than he'd been in long years.

As was Vikar, no doubt. By now he must have sated himself on Alvilda at least once—something Starkad's brother had longed for since he'd first laid eyes on the girl. And good for him—Agder needed royal children to establish a strong dynasty. Despite the dvergar, this land might yet prosper.

It might have done better under Starkad, but that was not urd, it seemed. No, nor was it his fate to claim immortality, though he'd been so close. Ironic, Vikar had cost him that, as well.

Though he'd shut his eyes, Starkad had not realized he'd slept.

At least until the fires started.

The smoke came first, filling the darkness. Choking him. Leaving him to wander in a drunken stupor, alone.

Wake up ...

Everything around him had grown empty, save for flames. Spreading fast, engulfing the woods through which he fled. The inferno chased him, ever gaining no matter how fast he ran.

Wake up ...

Starkad stumbled upon a root. The entire tree from which it jutted crumbled into ash.

He rolled over on the forest floor, as a shadow fell upon him.

A figure of smoke and flame, smoldering, like a fiend of Muspelheim come to burn away all creation.

Wake up!

Starkad jolted awake to the sound of battle. He stumbled out of the bed shelf, fell over one of the shieldmaidens, and slammed face first into the floor.

"What the fuck!" the woman complained. "Can't you even ..." She was sitting now, rubbing her eyes as Starkad tried to disentangle their legs. "That sounds like ..."

"Because it is!" he snapped. No time for his mail. Instead, he grabbed his swords and blundered through the door.

Being drunk was rewarding. Fighting drunk, less so. Waging war drunk ... was ill advised.

A bellowing man with an axe came racing down the hall. Blade raised for a killing blow. Moving so damned fast.

Starkad lurched back, just managing to get a sword up. The axeman ran straight into the blade, impaling himself. It stole his momentum right out from under him, and he pitched forward, dead almost instantly.

Well ... glorious. Right.

Still reeling, Starkad stumbled down the corridor into the great hall. Dozens of men lay dead. Dozens more engaged a raiding force that had broken into the wedding celebration. Shirtless and unarmored, Vikar wove his sword about, cutting down one man and then another.

With a roar, Starkad joined him. One of his blades took a man in the back of the neck. The other clattered off mail, his blow poorly aimed and ineffective save to throw the target off-balance. That was enough though, and Vikar chopped down into the man's skull, then kicked him away.

Behind Vikar, Harald lay on his face, empty eyes staring up at the ceiling. A gouge split him from neck to hip, and his blood and stinking guts had spread over the floor.

The king ... the king was dead.

The thought did not quite want to settle into Starkad's mind.

Grimacing, sobering fast, he engaged another murderer.

AT VIKAR'S SIDE, Starkad watched the burning longship vanish into the mist. Alvilda was clutching Vikar's arm, weeping without a sound.

"Those were Herthiof's men," Starkad said.

Vikar grunted.

Herthiof was just another petty king in Nidavellir, one more subject to the dvergar and no true enemy to Harald. Save that Harald had rejected Herthiof's son's proposal for Alvilda's hand. Maybe they had hoped to avenge wounded pride.

Perhaps though, Herthiof had set his sights on Agder and thought if Vikar was dead, he might claim the kingdom after Harald passed. Either way, only one course now lay open to Vikar.

Herthiof had slain the king, Vikar's father-in-law.

Naught less than total vengeance would do.

And that meant war. True war, the likes of which Starkad had not seen since they'd left Andalus.

In war, a man lost those he cared for.

Starkad was tired of losing friends and allies.

12

They had found Gylfi waiting in Ochilaik's hall. The sorcerer king was Odin's puppet, perhaps, but he was also wise, having lived years beyond that which was normally allotted to a man. And no king in Sviarland, no man, wanted Odin's voice as an enemy. Not even Starkad.

Much as Starkad had spurned Odin's order to serve Gylfi —and later learned Odin sent another ward to the king to earn Gylfi's loyalty—still he respected the man.

And so he had requested the king speak to him alone, and they had walked in the Fyris Woods, as Haki's men set about throwing corpses onto pyres lest the dead rise this night.

"We are much alike, you and I," the king said as they drew out of earshot from those engaged in such grisly work.

"Are we?"

"We have become instruments of a greater power. I accept my urd, but you resent yours ... from time to time."

Starkad groaned. "So you know what Odin did to me."

"What he did for you?"

That drew a chuckle. "Even now, I cannot say for certain whether he granted me blessing or curse."

"Such is the nature of the Art. If it works any benefit, it accompanies with an even greater price."

"It is ... the Art of which I wish to speak."

The aging king paused then and took to staring at Starkad from beneath the boughs of a withered ash tree. "It is not a path I advise to any man or woman. Once you look into the infinite blackness, you cannot unsee what is revealed. Nor worse yet, it will not unsee you."

"You mistake me. I do not seek tutelage in the Art." Though the ability to harness the Sight ... no. Before Starkad could even consider that, before he could go seeking the eitr, he must attend to the more pressing matter.

It should not have been his problem. It should not have ... happened.

But he had failed her.

And whatever it took to make that right ... well, he would do aught to assure her survival now.

"My friend suffered dire injuries in this battle. The völva cannot say if she will even live, much less that she will be whole again."

Now Gylfi groaned, the sound eventually becoming a mirthless chuckle. The old sorcerer leaned against a tree and slowly turned to look at Starkad. "You have no idea what it is you ask ... I am no god to deal out life and death on a whim."

Starkad glanced up at the setting sun. Even having such a conversation set his nerves on edge, much less having it in the failing light. It was not talk for men in darkness. Not talk for men at all.

"Can you help her or not?"

"Perhaps." Gylfi pushed off the tree, then spread his

hands. "Life might sometimes be stolen from one to give to another ... but there is always a price beyond that. A price to her, to me, to you ..."

"What price to me?"

"The vaettir will take what they will." The king shrugged. "But if you would have me risk mind, body, and soul to call upon them, I too must demand a hefty price."

"Name it. I will bring you silver or gold or aught else you desire, King. Give her back her life."

"Oh." Gylfi chuckled. "Even if my rituals work ... I cannot say she will be all she was. But regardless, I know what it is you seek in distant lands."

Starkad froze. No. Not that.

"And you will swear your oath to me ... that the next runeblade you retrieve shall fall into my keeping."

No. No! "Ecgtheow *already* brought you the runeblade of Thule!"

Gylfi shrugged. "And for the moment, it serves me to let him hold it. Though I might add, it was merely lost in Thule, not forged there."

"I don't care! The runeblade is *mine*, old man!" Starkad's hands started to rise to his swords. He forced his fists to close. To drop down. Gylfi was not his enemy. "It is mine."

"If you truly wish me to work the Art on your behalf, you must be willing to sacrifice aught you hold dear. And even then ... I offer no guarantees."

Starkad spit into a snow pile. This was not ... he could not ...

He had to have it.

He fucking *had* to have it.

Damn it. And Hel damn Odin, if the Ás had truly made Starkad into this.

He wanted to give Gylfi his oath. He wanted to ... but his

mouth would not work. It refused, even for Hervor, it refused to let him give up such wealth. "I ..."

"You must say the words."

And take a blade through his own gut in the process. No viler torture could befall him.

"I ..." The words wouldn't fucking come. No matter how hard he tried. He could not surrender such a treasure. Not *again*.

Gylfi nodded. "I rather thought not, Starkad. Hundreds of men and women died this day. We could not save them all ... and what makes one more deserving than another? You and I ... we have greater purposes, uses to which the Ás king holds for us."

And fuck Odin, too.

"I ... swear it! I swear the blade is yours. Save her!"

The king raised his bushy eyebrows. Finally, he nodded. "You surprise me. So be it, Starkad. I will do as best I can ... and we shall pay a price for it, all of us. I hope your ... friend ... is worth it."

She was ... though Starkad did not relish her suffering under the Art. As he had himself, so long ago ...

13

Twenty-Two Years Ago

The dead were piled up in Herthiof's hall. Blood drenched the floor, the tables, the walls. Blood and guts and shit all mixed together to fill the place with a stench that almost overpowered Starkad. He limped through the carnage, favoring his left leg after a lucky bastard had slashed his thigh.

"King Harald is avenged," Vikar said.

Starkad snorted. Yes, he imagined so. Herthiof was dead, as was one of his sons and many of his thegns. Some thirty men had died this night, not counting the seven Vikar had lost.

The rest of the men had set about looting, pillaging, some moving on to the village. Outside, screams rang out, as men burned and murdered and raped their way through Herthiof's villagers.

Vikar wiped his mouth. "You hear them shouting about trolls and vaettir?"

Starkad nodded. A surprise attack at night would do that

to men, make them think something out of the mist was coming for them. Very little amusing about that though. "So ... back to Agder."

Vikar turned about, still seeming to revel in the destruction. It had been a glorious battle, Starkad had to admit. A challenge worthy of song. The aftermath, though ...

A man behind them coughed, choking on his own blood. One of their own warriors, though Starkad didn't even know his name.

"Starkad," Vikar said after a moment. "Herthiof was king of Hordaland."

"And?"

"And also of Hardanger."

Huh. Starkad had not known that. Another petty kingdom already fallen to their now dead foe. He shrugged. "So there will be lands ripe for plunder for a few moons, yes."

"Plunder ... or conquest. I have taken Herthiof's kingdom—why should I not add it to my own, as he intended to do to Agder?"

Starkad groaned, then wiped sweat from his brow. "How far do you intend to reach, little brother?"

"All of southern Nidavellir, perhaps. Think of it ... Healfdene has united most of Reidgotaland. Why should I not accomplish the same here?"

"To prove to Odin and Tyr that they were wrong about you?" As if it might undo their long banishment. As if the apples would not still be denied to the both of them because Vikar could not follow orders.

"I don't have to prove troll shit to them! I will build my own empire here in the frozen north."

"The dvergar—"

Vikar scoffed and waved that away. "Will get more tribute than ever before and find themselves well sated."

Starkad nodded. Well, there never was any swaying his brother once he'd set his mind. "If you do this ... Herthiof's brother will surely come to claim what he believes his due."

"And will you fight for me, Starkad?"

Starkad snorted. "Did you really have to ask?"

THE WARS WENT on and on.

And they won, more oft than not. Starkad did as Vikar asked, championed him time and again. They fought Geirthiof, brother of Herthiof, and Starkad slew him. They claimed Telemark and the uplands. They fought Herthiof's son Fridthjof and Starkad's handpicked crew defeated him as well, forced him to surrender all his lands.

And the moons passed, as the south of Nidavellir fell into Vikar's hands.

Some, like the pirate King Gudlög, bowed willingly and offered tribute. Others Starkad put to the sword.

It suited Starkad well enough, he supposed. For as Vikar's fame spread, Starkad's spread faster. Men said he was so fast with a blade it was like fighting four different men. And thus, he fastened the name Eightarms.

All of it, Vikar took as his due.

And after so long, finally, they sailed home. Exhausted and on the cusp of a winter that seemed poised to be more brutal than any Starkad remembered.

And then the winds had broken.

And for nigh to a moon, they had found themselves becalmed and with too few men left alive to man the oars.

Starkad leaned over the gunwale, staring out into the

mist. Beyond, the mountains of Nidavellir rose high. Beneath those, the dvergar dwelt. And they had heard of Vikar's many conquests and had demanded higher and higher tributes. But to them, Vikar offered no argument. What they asked, he paid.

No man wanted to cross the vaettir.

Bones clattered upon the deck once again, as the völva made another throw. They had brought the woman to assure their victories. To help them foresee the will of the gods—and these people largely took to worshipping the Aesir, whose own fame spread like wildfire. Starkad did not bother to correct them. They would not have listened.

Finally, he stalked over to the völva. "Tell me, witch. When will the winds return?"

The woman looked up with haunted eyes. "There are ... unbelievers amongst the army."

Starkad barely contained his chuckle. Unbelievers, yes, and he was one of them. How would this woman react to hear that Starkad himself was born among the Aesir, that none of them had been gods before they took Vanaheim? That Odin's power came ... from a piece of a fruit?

A fruit—golden treasure more valuable any dug from beneath Midgard. Starkad dreamed of them, sometimes, the apples.

"You're saying the Aesir stole our winds because not all of us believe in them?"

She shrugged. "That I cannot say. But they will not help us unless we make a sacrifice in their honor."

By now, several other crewmen had gathered, Vikar included. The king scowled at his wise woman, until Starkad half expected him to sacrifice *her*, though no man would ever dare harm a völva. "Odin is doing this to us, then?"

A warrior groaned, and several others muttered.

"Well," Vikar said. "We cannot well march the army home by land through these mountains. Least of all with winter approaching."

"We must try the land," Starkad said. "We cannot winter here."

"No. We both know Odin is a right bastard. If he wants something from us, he'll have it, or we'll suffer twice over until we grant it."

Starkad folded his arms. He'd never told Vikar that Odin had pled with him to abandon his brother. He had, however, mentioned the king's request that they go to Gylfi. A request neither of them had honored.

"Besides," Vikar said after a moment. "Storms could crop up any day now. We don't make it home soon, we may not make it home at all. So ... how are we to decide it?"

"By lots," the völva said. "Each man will draw a rune, and I will hold one duplicate."

Starkad groaned. "You will leave our lives to chance?"

Vikar shook his head. "No, brother. I must leave them to urd."

VIKAR MUST HAVE THOUGHT himself doing right by his kingdom. Maybe he even wanted to placate Odin.

Chance, urd, or Odin's machinations—it was Vikar who drew the cursed rune.

So ... had the völva known? Had Odin? Or worse yet, had the king of the Aesir created this situation to punish Starkad?

"So be it, then," Vikar said. Starkad's brother was staring out at the sea. "We must make land on those shores. The völva says I must hang, as Odin once hung himself."

The tale of Odin hanging from Yggdrasil and returning from the dead sounded like fancy to Starkad, though Tyr swore it was all true. In any event, Vikar would not return from such an experience.

"Hold off on this mist-madness," Starkad pled. "Await the morning, at least. One more night ... then, if there is no wind ... then ..."

Vikar gripped the gunwale. "Suppose another man had drawn the unlucky lot, brother? Would I not then demand he face his urd? Can I ask less of my people than I will give myself?"

"You are not just one of the men. You are king. Your queen awaits you, thick with child. Do you not wish to see her again?"

Vikar spat into the sea. "Of course I do. But if I look upon her again, I must do so without shame."

"Wait. Just until the morn. I beseech you."

And at last, Vikar nodded.

THE OARS ROWED THEMSELVES, ferrying the tiny boat through the mist, carrying Starkad and Tyr. No moon graced the night and but few stars pierced the darkness. Tyr's face was shrouded, only the hint of his beard, his chin visible. But Starkad knew him.

"Where are we bound?" Starkad asked.

"To the Thing." Tyr spread his hands ... wasn't there something wrong with his right hand? It looked fine now.

"Am I to be judged?"

"We are all of us, always to be judged."

"By ..."

"... By the living and the dead. Always by the dead." Tyr's voice sounded off, scratchy and coarser even than usual.

On and on the boat drifted, propelled by unseen hands. And then it scraped up on ice, banked upon a small island in the midst of the empty sea.

Starkad rose.

Tyr was gone ... had not the man been with him?

Swallowing—for he could not deny the compulsion to walk forward—he left the boat and climbed the shore.

Upon a hill sat eleven chairs, a twelfth set amongst and above them. In each chair sat a shrouded figure, hands lit with etheric blue flame. Faces concealed.

"Where am I?" Starkad asked, finding his feet had carried him to the circle's center.

"Perhaps you gaze upon the thrones of fate." The speaker was in the high chair, and Starkad knew that voice.

"Odin?"

Another sitter spoke, this time to Starkad's left. "So concerned with Odin ... and yet you think to defy the will of Asgard?"

The ground trembled beneath Starkad's feet. Rocks tumbled down the hill. A crack rent the land separating him from Odin, sent Starkad stumbling back onto his arse.

This crack spread, bubbling darkness seeping from it. And swirling until it became a maelstrom of chaos and shadow. Wind tugged at Starkad's clothes, his boots, his ... soul. Pulled them closer and closer, with each passing moment.

"What ...?"

"Perhaps then," Odin said, "to defy the thrones of fate you might dive into the abyss of the Roil."

"What abyss? What the fuck is the Roil? Release me!"

Odin stood now, strode to the very edge of the maelstrom, though its winds ruffled his clothing not at all. "It is the darkness beyond the dark, waiting to devour body, mind, and soul. It waits, hungry. Eternal."

"You're not real! This is not real!"

All the figures had stood now. Their eyes gleamed in the darkness, luminous green, angry. Judging.

Odin shook his head, his face still concealed. "Reality is more tenuous than you might imagine. And while I fight to preserve our fragile world, you deny me ... but I am not given to wanton cruelty ... and might, beseeched by a father, be convinced to bestow upon the son a gift." Odin pressed his hand down into the maelstrom, and the shadows rent apart. They turned to dust and drifted up into the sky, vanishing into the blackness above.

"F-father? You mean Tyr?"

"You are forever denied the apple you so desired ... and yet, I cannot ignore the pleas he makes in my ear. Let you live, keep your youth, and grace this dying world as we do."

After several breaths to steady himself, Starkad rose. He'd be damned before he met Odin or anyone else lying on his arse on the ground. Even if this was a dream.

"You will grant me an apple?"

"It is too late for that. But I can yet offer you three lifetimes of man. I can call upon the darkness and grant to you years beyond the reckoning of men. And too, you will find great wealth, carry mighty weapons, and be ever victorious in battle. And you will ... be my sword in the world of men."

Starkad had thought his prize lost forever. But if he could not have an apple ... to have all Odin had promised ... was it possible? Long life and wealth and glory?

"What must I do?"

One of the men threw back his hood to reveal Tyr's face.

"Honor." The man's eye sockets were empty pools of blackness.

Another stood, this time revealing Starkad's mother's face, her eyes too missing. "Sacrifice."

A final figure strode toward him. This one dropped his cowl to reveal Vikar's face. "Blood. Of the one who cost you everything."

"YOU MUST COMPLETE THE SACRIFICE," Starkad said, as he and Vikar stood watching the dawn. "But let it be a mere gesture to placate the gods we defied."

Vikar turned away from the sun to look at Starkad. "How so?"

"A simple noose of calf intestines tied to a mere twig. Let the völva perform the ritual, you pretend to die … and then we might all sail from here."

His half-brother clapped him on the arm. "I hope you are right, though I find myself doubting we can so easily appease Odin."

Nevertheless, Vikar rowed them ashore himself. Starkad, two thegns, and the völva, all dour. While aboard the ship, the men watched the king going to his mock death. Even knowing it not real, they feared. They feared the wrath of Odin for the deceit, perhaps, or feared more to lose the beloved ruler who had led them to victory after victory.

Ashore, Starkad was the first out of the boat. "I must find a calf or goat or something else. We need the intestines for the … sacrifice."

Vikar nodded. "Do not take long, brother."

Starkad flinched at the word. Brother? Half-brother, and though he'd loved Vikar dearly … surely his brother knew what had to happen. Urd had been declared ... Odin must be appeased. Vikar himself had said so, had accepted his role in it. He'd been planning to go willingly before Starkad had talked him down yesterday.

And now ...

That dream ran through Starkad's mind, over and over. Ceaseless and undeniable.

The rope was waiting, where the dreams had said it would be. When Starkad hefted it up, it became slick and slippery—a calf's intestine. As Odin had promised.

Vikar knew. He must know. He had accepted this.

One way or another, Odin would have his due ... and this way, Starkad might claim all he'd forsaken in order to join Vikar these past years. He might ...

Be damned.

He blew out a long breath. This had to happen.

It had to.

Odin was offering him something close to immortality. Offering the next best thing to the prize Starkad had been denied because of Vikar. Been denied, so Starkad's little brother could become a king.

As Starkad returned to camp, he found Vikar standing atop a rotting stump. A tiny branch overhung this, flimsy and leafless in the winter.

Starkad flung the intestines at the feet of a thegn, who then tied it over the branch. With a glance at Starkad—and he nodded, damn him!—Vikar tied a noose and set it round his neck.

"Vikar ..." Starkad started to say.

His brother stepped off the stump. And it crumbled to dust beneath him. The flimsy branch thickened, twisting and growing, shooting out like a spear. And the calf's guts became a rope. The noose jerked tight around Vikar's throat.

His eyes latched onto Starkad's.

Had he known?

Had he *known* and gone anyway?

The men stood in shock as their glorious leader died. As their dreams of a united Nidavellir died with him.

And then came the shouts of kinslayer. Of betrayal. Of murder.

The blood sacrifice Odin had demanded.

Vikar's thegns drew their blades, cursing Starkad.

And as Starkad killed the two thegns, he knew—Odin had called for their deaths as well.

14

*E*very breath brought fresh pain. Agony that lanced through her lungs. It cut through her throat. It sent tiny bolts of lightning coursing up and down her arm, her shoulder, her side. It hurt so much she wanted to close her eyes and cease to breathe.

Trying not to breathe hurt even more.

Hervor hated life.

But she sure as Hel did not want to die.

She lay in a closed room, lit only by a tiny fire pit. Someone had bandaged her wounds with a foul-smelling poultice. Perhaps it lessened the pain. If so, she could not imagine how it might have felt without the rank stuff.

Word had come that Haki had killed Ochilaik. Had hunted down the Yngling king's sons. Had proclaimed himself king of Upsal. So ... the Yngling dynasty had fallen. Was her oath ... truly fulfilled? After three years of blood and sacrifice and betrayal and lies ... had she succeeded?

Perhaps at the cost of her own life. Her whole body seemed ready to give out. How was she even yet still alive?

She'd seen men die of lesser wounds. Bleeding inside, choking on their own blood.

That ought to have been her urd.

But here she was, still alive in her unending agony. A surprise.

She lay there a long time. Alone. She had to piss but dared not try to sit up on her own.

Finally, she called out for help.

Here she was ... mighty warrior. Famed and feared and wielding a runeblade. Begging a servant to help her use the godsdamned chamber pot.

After such wounds ... no. She might never be a warrior again.

Hel, maybe she'd never even be able to do as Grandfather had wished and bear children.

Assuming she lived long enough to even return to Ostergotland.

It was neither servant nor slave who came in, though, but King Haki himself. And she wasn't going to ask *him* to help her piss. "My king."

He sat down beside her, watching as he did so. Careful not to disturb her. He offered her a skin of mead. "Slowly. Just a sip, now."

Hervor took it with her left hand and did take a very small swig. That hurt too. Almost choked her. Coughing, she handed it back. "T-thanks."

"You were right, Hervor. We won because of Starkad. I'm indebted to you. What would you ask of me?"

"I ... uh ... I suppose give the reward to my grandfather." And what would he do with it? Hoard it a few years until he died as well. Was he right, back when he'd pled with her to stay, to rule, to carry on their family line? The men of Bolmso were all dead, her father's line destroyed. And now her mother's line would end too. All of Hervor's kin, gone forever.

Wiped from Midgard.

"He will be my friend as long he lives."

Oh. Even Haki realized Grandfather had not so much time left.

"I'm going to die?"

"Huh." Haki rubbed his forehead. "You were fortunate, I suppose. King Gylfi was visiting the new king of Upsal when we arrived. As a gesture of goodwill, the king prepared this poultice for you, and our völva wrapped your wounds."

She feigned a smile. The worse wounds lay inside, and they both knew it.

Haki nodded. "Gylfi did some strange, unmanly things to keep you alive. He says with luck you might pull through. I suppose it means I must maintain peace with Dalar, after he showed such kindness to my thegn."

Well then. Living, even in pain and unable to wield a sword ... it was better than death. It was better than waking up at the gates of Hel. She supposed.

But Haki didn't leave.

"There's something else?"

"Hmm. You called Starkad Eightarms your friend. Apparently he quite thought so, as well. He asked Gylfi to use his Art to help you."

"Use magic?" A pit opened in her stomach. All she had ever seen of the Art was dark and foul and born of Niflheim and Hel. The power it represented corrupted and destroyed. It had, if she understood, cursed Starkad. And yet he was willing to invoke it?

"Gylfi is a sorcerer of some repute. He claims he could call upon vaettir that might aid you ... but it would cost him."

"W-what did he ask for?" What *could* the sorcerer ask for that would so throw Haki into doubt?

"I do not know. That was between Starkad and the king of Dalar." Haki shook his head.

She had heard sorcerers dealt in souls and life itself, in things irreplaceable. That their prices defied imagination.

Hervor had trouble swallowing. "So …?"

"Gylfi says the moon will be full in two nights. That's when he intends to work his Art. They will take you … into the woods. Neither does Gylfi wish to practice his ways here, nor would we have it in our town."

"And I'll be able to fight again?"

Haki turned to her now, brows drawn so tight his forehead had more creases than she'd ever seen in it. "I don't know, Hervor. I have no idea what will happen. Save that he intends something dark … and your friend is willing to pay a hefty price to get this done. I pray to Odin this course is wise."

IN THE EVENING, Starkad came to her. He sat on the bed where Haki had sat, the look on his face again unreadable. What exactly went on in that head of his, anyway? Hervor could rarely tell.

She waited for him to speak.

After a moment, he sighed. "I should have been faster."

"Huh?"

"On the battlefield. Maybe you would not have been hurt if I had dispatched my foes more quickly."

"Oh." Hervor grunted. "So you mean you're an idiot."

"What?"

She wanted to cuff him on the head. Of course, she

could barely fucking move. "Were you the only warrior in those woods? The only person fighting for our cause? I do not ask for you to *defend* me! I am ... I was ..."

Useless ...

Starkad nodded. Rose. Paced about the room looking like he didn't know what to do with his hands. "So. I'm leaving tomorrow."

What?

But Haki had said Starkad had bargained with Gylfi to try the Art upon Hervor. So what was he about now?

She frowned, saying naught. Surely there was more to this.

"There is something I require before I can go to Glaesisvellir ... and I must have that runeblade. Volund assured me I would find it among many other treasures lost somewhere in the kingdom of Godmund."

Now Hervor grimaced. What was this? He bargained for her to be restored—which sounded impossible—but he planned to leave before seeing it through? What the fuck was wrong with him?

Moreover, if he felt so compelled to go after this blade, he ought to ask *her* to come with him. After all, Hervor had been the one to claim the runeblade of Thule.

Starkad stared at her face a moment, then nodded. "Rest, shieldmaiden. Perhaps we shall meet again on my return."

And then the bastard just left.

Hervor lay there, mouth agape, trying to fathom what had just happened.

As HAKI HAD SAID, men came to carry Hervor out into the Fyris Woods. Every step of the way had sent fresh jolts of pain shooting up and down her arm, her neck, her chest. It grew so bad, she shut her eyes, tried to block out all thought.

The mist was thick this evening, though, and she could almost feel the dead. Men had burned the corpses, of course. Everyone feared draugar. But the ghosts of the battle seemed to linger, watching, hateful of the living who betrayed them.

Or maybe she was just delirious with pain.

At Gylfi's instructions, the men laid her upon a mossy clump beneath a withered tree, deep in the wood. Then they fled, their faces pale and fearful as maids. Not from the dark, probably. Maybe not even from the ghosts that surely haunted this place.

Gylfi himself was weathered, his hair and beard long and gray, great creases marring his eyes. The old king seemed just a little like her grandfather, in his way, though he did have a greater air of power about him. An air of ... mystery, perhaps? Of something ever so slightly off about him.

He puttered about, inspecting all the local trees. Eventually, he opened a large bladder that stank of blood. The thing was nigh to as big as her head ... and it was filled with blood. Human blood? Shit. What vileness was he about?

Hervor cleared her throat. "I ... will be able to fight again, after this?"

Gylfi grunted, dipped two fingers in the blood, and drew a rune upon a tree. Finally, he turned back to her. "Perhaps. Evoking vaettir is ... imprecise. They may heed my call, and if they do, they may do as I have asked. Or they may do aught else they wish here. No being of the Otherworlds has our best interest at heart." He resumed painting the odd runes. "In truth ... I think they hate us, the living. They torment us in the worst ways they can think up."

"Then why do it?"

Again he paused. "What? Sorcery?" A long sigh escaped him, like he could barely stand the answer himself. "Oh, child ... because once you have looked into the darkness ... it never lets you go back. So we struggle to control it, failing as oft as not."

Hervor shuddered at his words, even that movement hurting all the more. After a moment, Gylfi stuck a pair of torches on either side of her body. They offered but scant warmth, but they did serve to keep the mist at bay—a small blessing.

He worked a while more, painting trees and rocks with symbols that meant naught to Hervor. Was it all show or did these things accomplish some end? The old man moved about slowly, clearly pained for his efforts.

Finally, Gylfi came and sat beside her, groaning as his back audibly popped.

Hervor wanted to look him in the eye but couldn't turn her head.

Gylfi clucked his tongue and stretched. "The problem with asking vaettir for aid—or even compelling it from them —they tend to extract a hefty price from ... everyone."

"Everyone?"

"The one calling upon them. The one receiving their ministrations. The one who requested it. Sometimes those nearest to those people. These beings are steeped in cruelty and capriciousness beyond the ken of mankind. And they lie. Always." He breathed out a long breath. "You know, shieldmaiden, you remind me of a ward I raised not so very long ago. Brave and strong, a warrior. I, uh ... well, it makes what I must ask of you more uncomfortable."

Oh, she did not much like the sound of *that*. "Speak, old man."

"I must remove your shirt, Hervor, and paint the runes upon your injuries."

Uh huh. Lecherous old fuck. Did his sorcery really require that, or was it an excuse to ogle her tits? Not that it mattered, she supposed. In her current state, she could not have stopped him from doing aught he wished to her.

Of course, as he began to peel off her tunic, the way he had to twist her arm felt like getting kicked by a troll. It sent tears welling in her eyes. All Hervor could do was grit her teeth and try not to sob at the agony. Finally he let her lay back, half naked, vision blurred with the haze of pain.

She drew in deep breaths, those too feeling like they would tear her insides apart.

Gylfi cut away her bandages, gentle at that, at least. Then he pulled the bladder over, then began tracing blood over her clavicle, shoulder, arm, and ribs. Even his light touch hurt, and the blood had grown cold and clammy. His fingers brushed the edge of her right breast as he worked, but he seemed so intent on his designs as to hardly notice.

Maybe he'd spoken the truth about taking no pleasure in this. Small comfort though that offered.

"I have a tonic that will put you to sleep."

"Sleep?"

"It primes your mind and body to receive the ministrations of vaettir. And ..." Gylfi glanced around. "Most would prefer not to see direct influence from the other side of the Veil. It cannot be unseen. It is ... unlikely you will enjoy the dreams, though."

Oh, wonderful. Hervor glowered at the old man. "Just do it."

He produced a ceramic vial from his satchel, uncorked it, and tilted it up to her lips. The stuff stank like horse piss. Tasted worse. Oily and slick.

Hervor coughed, sputtering.

She felt naught at first, save perhaps a slight dizziness.

And then she shut her eyes.

※

It was the most crowded market Hervor had ever seen. Streets clogged with strangers. Dark-skinned foreigners and locals alike, all buying, selling, shoving. Hawking wares.

All with black eyes.

All watching her.

"Come on, now," Starkad said. "We have to find the building they're keeping your grandfather in." The man disappeared into the crowd, wading through it like a river.

"W-wait," Hervor mumbled. Her mouth was thick, not working the way it ought to. So many people all looking at her.

Angry. Hostile. They hated her. Thousands of them, all staring. Blaming her for every ill of the world.

Why? What had she done?

"Starkad!"

The sun dipped below the horizon, the moon rising at the same instant. Clouds swirled overhead, crackling with thunder and unshed lightning.

A howling wind.

"Starkad!"

There, he disappeared through a doorway. A shop? A cobbler? Why would Grandfather be held in a boot shop?

Rough hands shoved her, held her back from the doorway. Groped her. Pushed her down into the dust. Heavy feet trod on her hands.

Her arm felt like it was on fire. Her whole shoulder, her lungs, were burning.

Screaming, she crawled forward, batting aside the face-less crowd. They formed up in a ring around her, staring down. Hissing like snakes.

Hervor managed her feet and stumbled through the doorway, falling up the stairs. Why were there stairs in a cobbler's shop? She pitched forward, landing on the shop floor. Starkad was there, haggling with Grandfather over a pair of boots. Arguing bitterly, shouting insults.

Starkad stood with his back to a massive window, floor to ceiling. Beyond that crashed a waterfall, stretching high into the night and disappearing into mist below. It roared in a cacophony that drowned out the sounds of the market below. It beckoned her ... to once again be sucked into oblivion.

"What the ...?" Hervor mumbled as she drew nigh.

"Honorless dog!" Grandfather shouted. And he shoved Starkad.

The man flailed, then plummeted backward over into the falls.

"Starkad!" Hervor shrieked. She rushed to the window, but he was gone.

The stairs! The stairs must lead down there. She'd search the crowd until ... a chill wind washed over her, prickled her bare flesh. She was ... naked?

Shit.

She couldn't rush out into the crowd without clothes. Where the fuck had her clothes gone?

She turned about, but the shop was empty. Except for boots. Boots watching her with their lidless, watery eyes.

A scream caught in her throat. The boots were after her.

Panting, hardly able to run straight, she stumbled down the stairs. They opened out into a dense marsh ... like the

Fyris Wood. A deep night had settled over it, and she could make out less than five feet ahead of her.

"Starkad!"

Her bare feet squelched in the mud beneath her.

Crickets chirped. Unseen frogs croaked.

Hervor pushed on. Tree roots writhed and twisted like serpents.

The bog bubbled, like pools of viscous shadows, seeping darkness into the world. So black she feared to look inside. It would devour her.

Her heart was pounding against her ribs so hard it was going to burst through them. Hervor ran, trying to scream. Unable to get it past the lump in her throat.

In the path ahead, a tree split down the middle with a sound like flesh rending.

A heavy heartbeat.

Thump thump.

From within this tree erupted red light the color of inflamed skin. Something bubbled out of the rift like pus, taking the shape of a woman. Naked, lithe. Her flesh black and gray, bark-like. Her eyes glowing green with Otherworldly light.

Hervor collapsed onto the path. Serpentine roots lashed out at her, wrapped around her ankles. She shrieked.

The roots jerked her forward, dragged her closer to the emerging woman.

Hervor clawed at the ground. Her fingers dug into the mud but found no purchase, only drawing deep rivets along the path.

The creature—ash-wife?—stepped out of the tree and strode toward her, licking her lips.

Shrieking, Hervor swung at the ash-wife. Tried. But her right arm wouldn't work. It hung limp at her side. The ash-wife grabbed Hervor by both biceps and hefted her up. Shoved her back against the rent tree. Vines lurched out of it and wrapped around Hervor's wrists. Pulled them tight.

Sucked her arms into the pus-filled opening.

Hot and damp and awful.

Squishing.

Squelching.

The ash-wife leaned in close to Hervor's face. An over-long, bulbous tongue lolled out, and the vaettr licked Hervor's face. The slurping tongue lanced over Hervor's body, between her breasts. Down. Between her legs.

Hervor writhed, spat at the vile creature. "Get off me!"

"Do you know what we miss?" The creature's voice was lush, full like the moon, like the wild. Almost seeming ready to burst. "Do you know why so many bargains are sealed thus?"

Odin preserve her ... "Sealed ... how?"

"Oh. You know."

Another tree rent across the path, this one cracking like thunder. From it stepped a ... man. If you could call the wood creature that. Male. Clearly, given his erect cock.

Hervor grimaced. "Fuck you! Get away from me."

"It is your ... dream." The ash-wife's tongue slurped all over Hervor's exposed flesh as the male stalked closer.

Well, Hel. If it was just a dream ... "Then fucking do it!" Hervor bellowed at him. "You think you have what it takes? You think that pathetic excuse for a cock can get the job done? Well then just—"

The creature surged forward and grabbed her hips. His fingers became like roots. They dug through her flesh, burrowed into her gut. Through the haze of pain, she barely even noticed his *other* intrusion.

And then the ash-wife bit Hervor's broken clavicle. Her

teeth bored into Hervor like dozens of maggots. Sucked the blood and life and very soul from Hervor.

And Hervor screamed and screamed and screamed.

&.

"HERVOR!" Gylfi was shaking her.

Hervor lurched forward. Her fist caught the king in the jaw and sent him sprawling. "Fuck you! Fuck you, old man."

Gylfi rolled over, rubbing his face. "It was ... a dream. Whatever you saw, it wasn't real."

Her heart was still trying to beat right out of her chest. "It felt godsdamned real."

He rose, shook himself. "Don't most dreams?"

She looked down at herself. Still naked but only from the waist up. And she was sitting. Her arm and shoulder still hurt like Hel, but she could move them. For that matter, breathing had gone from agony to merely painful.

Grunting with the effort, she too rose. It had worked?

She snatched up her shirt, but when she tried to don it, her right shoulder still wouldn't bend all the way. Trying left her gasping with pain, almost brought her to her knees.

"Your healing has been accelerated, aided beyond what nature might have allowed. Nevertheless, I hope you did not expect a full recovery."

Hervor grimaced, then jerked her tunic on as best she could. Finally, after catching her breath, she turned on him. "I did not expect to be *violated* by ... by whatever the fuck that was!"

"The draught I gave you is known to cause horrific hallucinations. A necessary side effect of the process."

She hesitated. "So ... none of what I saw was real? You're

saying all of that came out of my own head?" If so, she was even more disturbed than Grandfather had ever thought.

Gylfi clucked his tongue then shook his head. "Most people ... prefer to believe so. I have ... always tried to tell myself the same after such traumas."

So the king ... had also experienced the ... violations? Two possibilities—either the draught pulled the most horrific tortures she could imagine from her own mind ... or actual vaettir tormented her in her dreams. Gylfi said vaettir hated mankind. Hervor wasn't quite certain whether to be more afraid that beings of such malevolence watched her from just beyond the world she could see ... or that her own mind could produce such depredations.

Gylfi had said everyone involved paid a price for calling upon sorcery. Hervor had paid ... Gylfi must have. Maybe even Starkad.

Starkad ...

Whatever he'd offered Gylfi, he'd done it for Hervor's benefit. So then ...

Only one thing left to do.

She had to push hard, try to catch him before he reached his newest destination.

15

*G*ylfi's court had long been the center of Sviarland, at least as far as Ecgtheow was concerned. Some claimed the Yngling dynasty at Upsal was the strongest family ... or had been. Some moons back, Jorund and his brother Eikkr had fled here, fled from their own cousin Ochilaik who had claimed the throne. And plunged the whole damned kingdom into war to do it.

In weakening Upsal, Ochilaik had given Dalar its chance to seize control of all Sviarland. King Gylfi, however, had not seen things that way. The aging king had returned some few days back with word that now Ochilaik was dead and King Haki of Ostergotland had seized Upsal. And worse still, Gylfi had made an oath of friendship with him.

The old king had lost any taste for war, Ecgtheow supposed. The man reclined on his throne now, drenched in shadow and watching the drinking and cavorting of his men. Armed with the runeblade—Naegling, Gylfi called it —Ecgtheow might damned well have led the king's forces to countless victories. Instead, he sat at home and watched the king wither away.

Ecgtheow threw back the drinking horn, then passed the empty thing to a slave, finally tromping over to the throne.

Jorund eyed him as he passed, clearly bitter over all that had befallen his dynasty. Ecgtheow had limited sympathy. The man had lacked the stones to fight his cousin and so had fled like a craven. His urd was his own making.

And now, of course, Upsal was no longer even in the hands of the Ynglings. Jorund's whole dynasty had fallen.

"My king," Ecgtheow said. No one drew too close to Gylfi's throne. The king was long rumored to have touched the unmanly arts of the Otherworlds. And, combined with his volatile temper, well ... not even Ecgtheow would have considered showing the merest hint of disrespect. Odin alone knew what fell powers Gylfi might call upon if sufficiently irked. "The journey seems to have agreed with you."

The king looked up at him, half his face still shrouded and thus hard to read. "Meaning?"

Ecgtheow fought the urge to squirm. "You seem ... enlivened with fresh vigor. Perhaps we ought to consider all of us going out for raids in the summer. Or even ..."

"Conquest?" The king scoffed. "I have no interest in conquest of Sviarland while our colony in Holmgard is faltering. While other lands have yet to embrace the light of the Aesir. If I were to turn my eyes elsewhere, perhaps it would be to Kvenland. Perhaps even a harder push into Bjarmaland."

Ecgtheow ran his tongue over his teeth. "Dalar has no easy access to either land, my king. The other kingdoms of Sviarland block our way. If Jamtla or Upsal were to fall under our sway, though, perhaps your plans could ..."

The king's glower stilled his words. "I have pledged friendship to King Haki."

Indeed. More was the pity. Ecgtheow was not going to win this debate. No one changed Gylfi's mind when he set about something. No one save maybe Odin himself or Gylfi's former ward, Sif. But no man knew what Odin said to Gylfi, and Sif had gone back to her real family some few years ago. It left a stubborn king who did not heed his thegns, nor even his daughter or grandson.

With a grudging nod, Ecgtheow slunk away and found a table away from the throne. Boredom must kill as many men as the mist. And Ecgtheow was godsdamned bored while Gylfi wasted this opportunity to enrich the fortunes of Dalar.

"My lord," Olof Sharpsighted said as Ecgtheow passed. "Long years I have served you."

"Indeed."

Ecgtheow sunk down before Jorund but looked at the other thegn.

"I find myself now eager to increase my fortunes," Olof said.

Gylfi ran a thumb over his bushy brow, saying naught else.

"The dynasty of Nidud has fallen, and Njarar has no king. With your blessing ... I would take my chances there. And should I succeed, my lord ... you know you'd have my eternal gratitude."

The king leaned forward just a hair, fixing Olof with a long gaze Ecgtheow knew firsthand to be most discomfiting. No man could long endure it without squirming. Olof, for his part, did well enough.

"You may go," Gylfi said at last. "Take your war band, and try your fortunes ... and may Odin walk at your side."

What? Ecgtheow balked and sputtered. So ... Gylfi

refused to make war himself, but he'd offer his blessing to another man who wanted to? Why? Why would he ... ?

Jorund leaned forward and drummed his fingers upon the table, drawing Ecgtheow's eye. "I know what you must be asking yourself."

"And?"

Jorund shrugged. "The answer is obvious, my friend. The king wants allies in positions of power, but he does not want to risk his own kingdom over this."

Ecgtheow scoffed. But ... was Jorund right? Did Gylfi actually want those loyal to him to claim the varied thrones of Sviarland? So. The king would not act himself nor risk bringing the wrath of the Ynglings down upon Dalar ... because a war between the two kingdoms threatened to destroy both. Threatened to weaken all of Sviarland.

Finally, he shook his head. "It matters naught. I have but a small war band loyal to me, and Olof has already claimed the only kingless kingdom in Sviarland."

Jorund glanced about him. "We could always arrange to *make* another land kingless, you and I. You carry a runeblade, do you not? Your fame as a warrior precedes you, Tiny. I would welcome you into my service, should you be so willing."

And if Ecgtheow helped Jorund reclaim the throne of Upsal, a man with every reason to be grateful to Gylfi and Dalar would rule the most powerful kingdom in Sviarland. And two kings would find themselves indebted to Ecgtheow himself.

So ... walk away now. Or walk into the fire and get all he'd hoped to claim. Fame and glory for himself and security for Dalar. Not a hard choice.

And Jorund must have read it on his face. He indicated

the man next to him, a warrior, though from the creases around his brow, he must have had ten winters on Jorund or Ecgtheow. "This is Hrethel, one of the few jarls who remained loyal to me when my cousin betrayed us. He and his people fled Upsal at my side."

Hrethel clasped Ecgtheow's arm with a firm grip. "We've been building our forces these past moons. Sending for allies, hiring what mercenaries we can afford. With your help, we might be ready to march on Upsal in a few days."

"Now?"

Jorund nodded. "We catch them just before the brunt of winter, and they'll never expect it. Haki thinks himself secure, may not even realize my brother and I yet live. Our spies tell me his champions have set about raiding, hoping to claim some last plunder before winter sets in. Even his brother has gone south, to Skane, intent over some bitch he met there."

Ecgtheow grunted. "And where is your brother now?"

"Eikkr is with our forces in the woods," Hrethel said. "But he can be ready to move as soon as we are."

Ecgtheow pressed his palm into the table. This was it. This was his chance at true glory and the riches that would come with it. "And what will your friendship be worth … should you claim the throne?"

"As much wealth as you can desire," Jorund said.

Hrethel nodded at him. "Trust us, brother. I will grant you a swath of land by the sea. Fields that can grow crops, space to fish. A fine place to raise your family."

"I am not yet married."

Hrethel shrugged. "Not difficult for a wealthy, landed man to find a bride."

Ecgtheow glanced at Gylfi. The king of Dalar had never

offered him aught so tempting. Well, maybe putting Jorund on the throne served Gylfi, maybe it didn't. But it sure seemed a chance Ecgtheow could not pass up.

And so he nodded.

16

*E*vening had drawn nigh, but still Hervor pushed on. Traveling in the dark carried so many risks, not least among them losing Starkad's trail. But it was the only way she'd ever overtake him.

She passed north, beyond Dalar and into Jamtla. She had raided these lands by sea, once, but never travelled by sled before. Not this far north. The chill deepened with each passing day. How far did Starkad intend to trek? Already he had veered off into the mountains, towering peaks that dwarfed the crags farther south. Did he intend to press farther, into Lappmarken? Beyond?

And then, even as darkness settled around her, the light of a campfire broke through the mist.

Starkad sat there, staring at her as she drew nigh. His face masked in shadow, scraggly hair hanging loose.

Hervor pulled the sled to a stop, untied the dogs so they could hunt, and then slumped down by the fire.

"You should not have followed me."

So still a bastard. That was all right. "You asked Gylfi to ... to ..."

"To use the Art to give you back your life. Not so you could throw it away up in these mountains or the deeper places I must go below them."

Hervor sniffed, her gaze settling on the hare he had roasting over the flame. The thick scent of it made her mouth water.

Starkad glanced over at it. "I'm certain it is ready by now." He pulled the spit away, then dumped the steaming flesh onto a clay bowl. "Help yourself."

Hervor snatched it up. The heat singed her fingers, forced her to drop the meat. She sucked on her thumb a moment, then sliced at the hare with her eating knife, letting steam out. "I heard a story once ... that Odin himself used the ... the Art on you. Extended your life."

Starkad grunted. "Heard that story too."

"Do you have *any* idea what I went through when ... when Gylfi ..."

"Dreams? Hallucinations?" Starkad yanked off a leg from the rabbit, blew on it, then took a bite. "Some people claim it's not even real. Just all brought about by herbs and poultices and foul smoke." Bits of grease dribbled down his chin and beard as he spoke. "Some of us know better. I've heard only a handful of true practitioners of the Art yet walk the world. True sorcerers I mean, not völvur meddling with their brews and weeds and shit. The Niflung sorcerers of Samsey. The witch-queens of Pohjola. A few wandering wizards scattered amidst the lands. So rare, the Art almost seems mere fancy to most folk. But you and I ..." He paused to bite off another hunk of meat. "We've seen things most men couldn't dream up in their worst nightmares."

"Niflungar ... draugar ..."

Starkad spit out a bone. "Naught good ever came from

the Art, I think. Except maybe that you're up and walking again."

Hervor too tore off some meat and chewed it while trying to pick her next words. "I know what I went through for that. Whether born of drugs or vaettir, I'd call that nigh to the worst experience I've ever ..." She shook her head.

Starkad nodded, obviously needing no elaboration. So he had been through something like that. Maybe Gylfi was right—maybe it was better to assume it wasn't real.

"I know what I went through," she repeated. "But I do not know what you bartered to achieve this—" she indicated her still sore right arm.

"It doesn't matter."

"It matters to me."

"Hervor ... let it be."

"No. Tell me what you gave Gylfi."

"Hervor ..."

"Tell me, godsdamn it! You did this for me—I have a right to know!"

Starkad poked at the rabbit but did not break off any more. "Skofnung."

"What?"

"The runeblade lost in Glaesisvellir. I swore to retrieve it and see it handed to Gylfi."

Now Hervor balked. Giving up the last runeblade to Tiny had driven Starkad into fits by all she could tell. And he'd willingly bartered away another one. Because of her. All the more reason she had to help him get it. He'd made an oath for her ... and honor demanded she aid him in upholding it.

"I'm coming with you."

"It's too dangerous."

"And I'm getting my fair share of the treasure. You were

right ... we got shit from Thule. So now I'll make my fortune off Glaesisvellir, and we both go home wealthy."

"You should return to your king ... or better yet, to your family."

Hervor tried to cross her arms over her chest, but her right one ached from the motion. She grunted.

"Oh," Starkad said. "You cannot even fight, can you?"

She spat out into the darkness, then glared at him. "You damn well know I can. *You* can fight with both hands. I'll learn too."

"I learned that from a man who lost his sword hand—but it took a long time to master."

She shrugged. "Maybe I'm a better student than you were."

He snorted at that. "Maybe. Eat the hare." He also tore off a bit more.

"Do you even know where we are bound?" Hervor asked.

Starkad grunted, then dug through his satchel. He pulled out a dried animal skin, marked with charcoal drawings. A map, hastily drawn, and yet with surprising eye for detail.

Hervor leaned in closer. A particular mountain, a slope of it indicated on the hide.

Starkad tapped a finger on the map. "I believe we are here." He indicated a mountain in the distance. "And that would make the upper slope there our destination."

Through the mist and darkness, Hervor could not make out a slope or much of aught else. Starkad clearly saw better than she did ... or was so driven by his obsessions he thought he did. She licked the rabbit grease off her fingers, then washed it down with a skin of water. "You said you expect to find a dverg ruin, yes? But we draw nigh to Nidavellir where we might find actual godsdamned dvergar. What is it you seek down there that is worth such a risk?"

He hesitated, then he shook his head. "Whatever we find ... follow my lead."

§▲

HER BREATH CAME heavy as she ascended the slope. The path was steep, slick with ice, and treacherous, even with crampons fitted on her feet. Once again, traveling with Starkad, she found herself climbing a frozen mountain. She snorted at the thought, the sound muffled by the scarf wrapped around her face, and then stolen by the frozen wind that kept howling over her.

That wind carried a light crop of snow with it, further obscuring vision and making the going even more tiring. Her right arm ached so she had taken to using a walking stick with the left. A chill sweat had built up under her clothes, and her mail felt frozen to her leathers.

None of that hardship bothered her so much as Starkad refusing to explain what he hoped to claim here. Why hold back? Why now? From all she had seen, he became this closed-lipped only when confronted about his mysterious past. Never willing to confirm or deny the supposed connections between himself and Tyr or Odin.

So did this dverg ruin somehow relate to that?

"Hervor!" Starkad called out from up ahead. "I found it!" The man stood a dozen feet above her, looking at the mountainside, though she could not follow his gaze from this angle.

At least they might soon be out of the wind and snow. She climbed farther, half pulling herself with the walking stick, before cresting a slight rise. Beyond that, the slope turned inward, into the mountain. A stone-pillared doorway framed a too-perfect tunnel descending into utter darkness beyond. Icicles descended from the top of the doorway like fangs from a serpent, and rime crusted everything, obscuring runes carved into the blocks forming the sides of the entrance.

Starkad yanked the scarf from his own face and stepped up to the threshold, spilling torchlight into the tunnel. "Before the rise of the Old Kingdoms, dvergar dug thousands of miles of tunnels across Midgard. Beyond even, some claim, into Utgard, perhaps even breaching into their own realm of Nidafjoll."

Hervor pressed up close to him. The flickering light only served to enhance the too-thick shadows inside. She couldn't make much out beyond about ten feet, if that. The path angled down almost as steeply as the slope outside had risen.

"Are you certain the dvergar are gone from this place?" she asked.

Starkad pulled a sword with his free hand. "I am certain of naught. We must assume the wretched vaettir still haunt these tunnels." He handed her the torch, and she took it in her right hand.

She had to hold it off to the side since raising it over her head was not an option. "So what will we find here?"

"If Wudga is right ... a manifestation of life ... and death, entwined."

17

*S*word in hand, Starkad pressed on down the tunnel, Hervor a half step behind him. Much as he wanted to scout ahead and keep her safe, he could not see without the torch she bore, nor fight at his full potential without being able to draw the second blade. Vikar's sword ... a weight on his shoulder.

A reminder of his failures.

Of his crimes.

Maybe one day, he'd replace his own sword with a runeblade. Vikar's he must carry forever. Such was the least he might do for his brother's memory.

The passage wound, twisting round like a coiling serpent, burrowing into the mountain. Already, they'd had to change the torch once. Now, he found himself wondering how long this trek would stretch on. Had he brought enough torches? They could not afford to be left in darkness here.

His ears popped as they continued downward.

"I can't say I much care for this place," Hervor mumbled.

Starkad knew he ought to feel the same ... and yet. His

pulse was thrumming here. Whatever was down here had rarely if ever been seen with human eyes. Such a thought was intoxicating. "You insisted on coming along."

Best then, if she did not spoil the moment with complaints. Whatever he *should* have felt about such delving, they served as a reminder—he yet lived.

"You ... enjoy this, don't you?"

Starkad flinched. How could she even tell that?

Instead of answering, he pushed a few steps ahead of her, darkness be damned.

The path finally leveled out, and along this route they walked, the only sound the soft plod of their boots, the crackle of the torch, the irregular pant of their breath.

The tunnel ended in a rectangular chamber, with stone doors set into the center of each of the other walls. Three possible passages, each carved with runes and symbols he could not read. Even assuming they could open doors with no obvious handles or mechanisms.

"What is this?" Hervor asked. She plodded closer to one of the walls, holding the torch over it.

And all but forcing Starkad to follow unless he wanted to pause and light his own torch. He stalked up behind her and inspected the marking over her shoulder. The door's seam was apparent, raised enough to make it obvious. The dvergar had not tried to conceal this passage, but how was he to ...

Hervor leaned the walking stick against the wall and ran her fingers over the stone, tracing the runes.

Maybe this would take a while. Clucking his tongue, Starkad dug another torch from his pack and began to light it, even as Hervor moved on to inspect another wall.

"There are other carvings beside the doors," she said.

"What?"

She knelt off to the side of one of the sealed exits, examining something close to the floor.

His own torch lit, Starkad joined her. The engraving had chipped and worn away over countless years but appeared to have once been a mural ... depicting twisted, shrunken bodies that must represent dvergar. Standing above them, on either side, were large numbers of men and women. Humans?

Starkad frowned.

"What does it mean?" Hervor asked.

"I'm not certain."

Legend said Volund had trained with the dvergar. Perhaps Wudga's father could have explained these ruins ...

Starkad moved on to the other door. Less dust coated this one ... someone had opened this passage more recently than the other. And those symbols ... he'd seen those.

He pulled the map Wudga had sketched from his belt. Yes, the man had drawn that same rune in the corner of the map. Starkad couldn't read aught, much less runes, so he hadn't given it much thought, but it looked just the same as the one in the center of this door.

He touched the symbol.

Naught happened.

There had to be some way past this damned door, though. "I don't suppose your runeblade can cut through stone?"

"I ... don't know. But either way ... I prefer not to draw it unless faced with immediate foes."

Starkad glanced at her, but she didn't explain herself. And he had no business pushing her, after all. After setting the torch down, he began pressing the door at every angle he could. Bits of stone and rock dust gave way under his efforts, but the door itself remained sealed.

Would have been useful had Wudga explained how to bypass this barrier.

Hervor, still inspecting the mural, had begun to crawl along the floor, tracing its path. Finally, she groaned and rose, her fingers trailing along the broken stone. "I think that ..."

She pushed on something in the design, and a faint click sounded inside the wall. Stone grated on stone as the door began to recede into the floor.

A curtain of dust poured from overtop it, sending Starkad backing away, coughing on the cloud.

He paused only to snatch up the torch and to draw a sword again. Then he pushed through the doorway into the next hall. This passage ran for a hundred feet before letting out into a cavern. The ceiling remained just above his head, some stalactites reaching down to not more than a foot above. The floor, however, dropped off beyond the range of the torchlight. A narrow ledge spiraled down around this pit, descending into the darkness.

Water dripped from some few stalactites, splashing down far below.

Starkad glanced back at Hervor, who nodded. Brave girl, he'd give her that. She might not enjoy these explorations as he did, but she'd not shy away from doing what had to be done.

Torch out to the side, he started down the slope. Slow, steady, watching his footing. The path was slick with water runoff. His boot skidded a little. No, he'd need to steady himself. Reluctantly, he sheathed his sword and used his left hand to brace along the cavern wall. That too was worn slick by the water. Cold and damp.

In fact, the whole place was chilled.

Taking gingerly steps, Starkad descended the path. After

a few moments, his torchlight began to reflect off mirror-like water below. He pushed on, until he made out what lay there. A circular pool dug into the floor, rimmed by carved stones, those too seeming rune-marked.

Hervor pressed up behind him, holding her own torch out over the gap to peer into the depths.

The waters were so still, she cast an almost perfect reflection in them, her torchlight seeming like a spreading flame below.

Around the edges of the pool, the shadows were so deep, Starkad couldn't make out much else. The cavern must overhang from the sides, blocking view. Otherwise, why wouldn't the light illuminate the land as well as the water?

He continued down the path until they reached the bottom. As he stepped off, the shadows seemed to recoil from his presence, seeping away like mist fleeing flame. Almost ... alive?

The darkness parted around him, but only just barely, only allowing him a bare few feet of light encircling him. And was this pool the eitr? If so, all he had to do was fill a skin with the stuff and they could be gone.

"I need to claim some of this liquid," he said. "But Wudga called it poison, so let not a single drop touch your skin."

"Why do we need poison?"

"If Wudga speaks true, this poison gives rise to life." Starkad pulled a skin and approached the waters.

Hervor snorted. "I heard the great tree, Yggdrasil, gives rise to life. So what does ..."

A slight ripple disrupted the water, even before Starkad had dipped the flask inside.

"Is there something *in* there?" Hervor asked.

Starkad had begun to kneel beside the pool but now

rose and fell back a step. "I don't know. Wudga mentioned something about—"

The waters ruptured, exploding in all directions. A serpentine head as big as Starkad's own burst from the pool, drawn upon a body that extended a dozen feet or more. Withered, skeletal wings dripping with ichor sprouted from the body, spraying the tainted stuff in all directions.

On pure instinct, Starkad tackled Hervor and drove her to the ground, out of the path of the waters. If they were poisonous ... he rolled off as soon as they hit the ground, pulling both swords off his shoulders in the same moment.

His war cry drew the serpent's gaze onto him. Away from Hervor. He had to keep it away from Hervor. She could barely fight anymore.

The creature lanced forward, its head shooting out like an arrow. Starkad fell backward, swinging his sword in an arc that clipped the dragon's maw an instant before it would have snapped down on him.

The creature recoiled the barest moment before lunging again.

And again Starkad swept a blade at it. The sword clattered off scales, halting the dragon's momentum but doing no visible damage to the monster. Damned thing was fast. He'd never keep this up for long.

The serpent hissed, baring fangs dripping with black venom. Its breath filled the cavern with a noxious stench like rotting flesh, leaving Starkad queasy, unsteady on his feet.

Trying to focus, he charged forward, one sword low, one high. The serpent surged at him, twisted to the side, avoiding one blade. It was smart. Not smart enough though. His other sword cleaved into the lighter scales holding its jaw together, spilling blood for the first time.

Shrieking, Hervor swung her runeblade at the serpent from behind.

Starkad had no clear view of her, but the serpent hissed furiously and whipped its body around so fast its coils slammed into Hervor and sent her flying against the cavern wall.

Her runeblade clattered away, lost in shadows somewhere.

Fuck.

Starkad used the distraction to press forward, raining blows upon the dragon's scales. Each clanged off ineffectively, no matter how much force he put behind them. The monster spun, revealing the gouge Tyrfing had torn along one side. Would that sword's venom kill even such a beast? Or was this creature born of poison?

Either way, he needed the runeblade. Eyes locked on the dragon that now met his gaze, Starkad edged around the pool. It had to be there somewhere. The monster did not stop him from reaching Hervor.

It bobbed ever so slightly, hissing. Eyes filled with hatred no mortal could fathom.

"Hervor ..." he said, pitching his voice low. He didn't want to alarm the ...

It lunged again, spraying more of the foul waters in the process.

No way he'd dodge it, so he leapt forward, sweeping both blades up in tight arcs. Each collided with the serpent, but this time, it did not pull back. It surged forward, its hot venom landing on Starkad's shoulder. His mail hissed as acidic poison corroded it, the stench almost enough to distract from the monster's own foul odor.

That was all he had time to think.

He tried to raise his swords again.

But the serpent darted around him, enwrapped him in its coils. Crushing weight pinned one arm to his side and stole the strength from the other. Vile waters seeped down over his head.

The coils tightened. Air exploded from his lungs as his body started to collapse.

His sword tumbled from limp fingers.

The serpent raised its head above him. Its maw opened, dripping more hateful venom. The jaw unhinged itself, opening that cavernous mouth too wide.

Like this ... ? The end ...

Everything started to grow hazy.

And then a shadow flew through the air, screaming.

Hervor's left-handed swing was clumsy. But then, the shieldmaiden had a large target.

Tyrfing bit into the dragon's body above where it held Starkad. Shearing through to the bone and halfway past it. Hervor landed in a heavy roll that sent her colliding with the wall.

The coils crushing Starkad loosened, ever so slightly.

A hint of air reached his lungs.

Gasping, panting for breath.

Everything going black.

CHILLS WRACKED HIM.

He knew he thrashed on a cold stone floor, but he could not open his eyes.

"Shh. Let the fire warm you."

A burning hand brushed his forehead.

WHEN HE FINALLY CRACKED OPEN his eyes, the torches lying beside him had both burnt down to mere embers. Hervor reclined across from him, her back propped against the cavern wall. Chest rising and falling in slumber, albeit tormented slumber from the look of it.

Starkad tried to speak, but his throat burned like he'd swallowed liquid flame.

He rolled over, managing a groan instead. She'd removed his shirt and mail, laid both nearby to dry. Patches of his skin had turned black. Bruises, in some places, by the feel. But elsewhere ... his flesh seemed half rotted. Where the waters had touched him?

Then how was he yet alive? Was it a side effect of whatever Odin had done to extend his life? Did it render him resistant to poisons?

"Hervor." It sounded more like a croak than speech.

But she opened her eyes and lurched over to him. "You're all right. When I saw your flesh I feared ..."

He would have as well.

The massive serpent lay sprawled over the cavern, still half submerged in the toxic pool.

He groaned. "Let's get what we came for."

"Indeed. I prefer not to sleep another moment in this vileness."

He could not have agreed more. This place was steeped in darkness and the Otherworldly. And though compelled always to seek out such places, to claim their riches ... Starkad had never benefited aught from the Otherworlds.

18

Twenty-Two Years Ago

*D*eep into the mountains Starkad had fled. The men of Adger hunted him for his crime, for his betrayal.

And it was a betrayal.

Starkad might try to blame Odin. He might claim Vikar had been ready to sacrifice himself, even. But Starkad had let his brother have hope—because Odin had told him to do it.

Maybe the Ás had simply wanted to see if Starkad would do it.

Oh, and he had.

He had slain his brother in the name of Odin's dark promise of darker sorcery. In the name of power and wealth and glory ... and all the petty things his wretched heart desired.

And in the night, the dreams had come.

Again and again, they came. Twisting in subtle variations upon the same, unending torment he had earned for himself.

MEN PURSUED him through the streets of some foreign city, all domed towers and strange arches and lattice-like stonework. Everyone in the town wore the same clothes— black robes, running with blood, dripping. And dozens of them dogged Starkad's every step. Relentless.

As he had been.

He ducked into an alley, but this merely opened back out into the marketplace once again. Always, back.

And they came on, offering the barest glimpse of their faces as they drew nigh. Vikar. They were all Vikar.

Always.

Starkad shoved his way through the crowd of black-robed Vikars. Each turned to him, let his wrathful gaze descend upon Starkad. Eyes dead and yet not empty, filled with loathing. Betrayal.

His heart tried to climb out of his chest and into his throat. It suffocated him.

A hand fell on his shoulder from behind.

Gasping for breath, Starkad spun on his pursuers. He swung a fist that seemed to move as if through water, lethargic and limp. Pointless.

Blood raced in his ears. Pounded against his temples. Dribbled from his mouth.

The blood of his treacherous heart.

His vision turned red. Hands closed around his throat and squeezed ... forcing his wretched heart back down into its rotten cage within his chest.

And all sight fled.

For a moment. The rocking of a ship jolted him awake.

And still, blood had crusted around his mouth. He tried to speak, but his voice fled, his throat parched, scratchy. A fit of coughing seized him.

Until hands again heaved him upward. Vikar stood there, his dead eyes staring into Starkad's own. He said naught. And no words would come from Starkad's mouth.

Over and over, he tried. Desperate to voice some apology.

"As if aught might make up for your crimes," Vikar said.

But Starkad hadn't meant it ... he hadn't meant for this to ...

How had he come upon this ship?

"For years you lingered here ... be it three or three hundred ... caught between life and death ... reaping the bitter rewards of your betrayal."

Starkad opened his mouth to protest. Blood dribbled out instead. Its coppery taste bubbled over his tongue. Choked him. His heart was again rising up into his gorge. Even it reviled him for his crimes, wanted to escape his wretched presence.

"Perhaps then, live the lives of three men ... and find victory. But not peace. Never peace ... never hope, never to sire children. Oh, deplorable brother. All your days will be drenched in blood and bereft of joy. Save that which flourishes only to be stolen away. You, who defy the bounds of nature ... and all filial bonds."

He didn't mean it.

He didn't mean it!

Starkad reached for Vikar's face, but his hands too were soaked in blood. His brother's blood.

Now, blood dribbled over Vikar's chin as well, bubbling

and dark. As his eyes gleamed with red light seeming to emerge from the gates of Hel.

Please. He just wanted to apologize. He hadn't meant it … he … he had *wanted* it …

Vikar spit in his face. Black phlegm and blood that stung Starkad's eyes, burning them like acid.

Backward, over the gunwale, Starkad toppled and fell and fell, plummeting through darkness.

A heavy impact threw up dust all around him. Choking him, clogging his nostrils. Seeping into his skin.

With trembling, bloody hands, Starkad tried to clear his vision. He lay … in a barrow … as the old men once built. The dead were piled high around him, the corpses of the betrayed and the betrayers alike.

All rotting together in never-ending anguish and grief and blood.

A single flickering torch sconce lit the room, its flame weak, hardly enough to banish the thick shadows engulfing the place.

And those shadows spoke.

"Long life."

"Victory in battle."

"Wealth."

The shadows danced about him, cackling and hissing and writhing in perverse pleasure at his horror.

Starkad's chest seized up. A biting pain tore through him.

A heart attack.

And he deserved no less.

He tore at his shirt, and it turned to dust, as did his trousers. All his clothes, his possessions, blew away on a wind that stank of rot and decay and old, old death. And still the shadows danced, the torchlight growing ever dimmer.

Tendrils of the darkness crept toward him. Screaming, Starkad swung his bloody fists at them, but his hands struck naught. The pain in his chest grew crushing. Drove him to his knees. Ribbons of shadows slithered ever closer.

They crawled up his skin like vipers, edging ever closer to his face. Cold, dead. The shadows penetrated the holes in his ears, filling his head with pressure. He squirmed and tossed about, to no avail. The vile tendrils wormed their way into his nostrils. Up his arse. Into his eyes.

His whole body spasmed in helpless agony as darkness saturated his twisted heart.

Or maybe ... the darkness had always been there. Waiting to come out.

And at that thought, the shadows were gone.

Starkad collapsed onto his hands, panting, able to breathe for the first time in centuries. For he must ...

"Embrace the darkness you have welcomed inside." The voice came from the shadows. Out of them strode Vikar, still clad in black robes. "You beckoned the dark into your heart, traded the light for years more of your life. Now, but one thing remains to you."

Again, Starkad's heart tried to climb up into his throat as he opened his mouth.

Vikar snatched Starkad by the hair, hefted him off the ground. His other hand darted down Starkad's throat, becoming viscous as the shadow tendrils had been. Horrible pressure felt like it would rip Starkad apart from the inside.

A crushing grip settled around his heart.

And Vikar jerked his hand out. In his palm rested Starkad's beating, blackened heart. "You have but ... to reap your rewards." And he outstretched his hand toward

Starkad. The heart sat there, oozing blood and pumping. Beckoning.

Unable to control his own hands, Starkad reached for it. Took it.

Warm. Pulsating. Strong and sinewy and wet.

He lifted it to his mouth.

"Do it," Vikar said.

Because he had embraced this path.

Because he had betrayed his own brother for power.

And Starkad bit down. His fang-like teeth tore through the thick muscle of his heart. Bitter copper filled his mouth.

And Vikar watched, eyes gleaming with crimson light.

Until Starkad ate every last bite.

And the torch finally flickered out, leaving him in total darkness.

AND AGAIN AND AGAIN, the dreams came. Reminding him of the price he had paid for his prolonged life. Had Odin known when he offered such a bargain?

He wanted to blame the Ás king. But lying alone, fearing to sleep, Starkad knew: he had no one to blame but himself.

Alone, Starkad wandered the mountains of Nidavellir, heading ever north. Into the wilds. For betraying his lord, for slaying his own brother, men would hunt him, wherever word spread of his crime. And Starkad was left with but one choice—keep fleeing ... and keep killing.

If he walked long enough, perhaps he might encounter the dvergar who ruled these lands. But thus far, Starkad had seen little sign of humans and no sign of dvergar. He'd heard the entrances to their dark halls oft lay atop mountain peaks, forcing humans to make treacherous climbs to offer tribute. An affectation or a deliberate cruelty, perhaps. In either case, he seemed safe so long as he kept to the valleys.

He passed into another such valley, seeded with evergreens and drenched in snows almost as heavy as the mountains flanking it. Here though, a thin plume of smoke rose about the mist. Starkad's supplies had dwindled to almost naught. He could hunt for food and clothing, but oil and rags for torches were other matters ...

Fire, most oft, meant humans, and he had not seen another human in long days.

And so he followed the smoke to a small cabin by a frozen stream.

For a time, he knelt behind a tree, watching. Just as he was about to approach, the door opened, and a woman emerged from the cabin. She was lithe, tiny even, with golden hair that seemed to reflect the afternoon sunlight.

Starkad snorted. Maybe he just hadn't seen a woman in overlong.

She trod over to the frozen river and knelt upon the ice, then began hacking away with an axe. Intent to catch some fish?

Well, maybe she'd let him help with that. Starkad made his way down toward her, taking care to move slowly and make just a bit of noise so as not to seem intent to sneak up on her.

The woman spun, revealing startlingly blue eyes that— for a bare instant—seemed themselves lit with sunlight as well. She leaped up, axe held out before her, and watched him approach.

"I mean no harm," he said, raising his empty hands in warding. "I am alone and ... hungry. I would very much like to share your fire."

The woman held the axe like a tool rather than a

weapon. No shieldmaiden, here, but neither did she seem overly frightened of him. Wary, perhaps. Finally, she nodded. "I'm Ogn."

"Starkad Eight ... Just Starkad."

She nodded, then glanced back at the river. "I was going to catch some fish for tonight." Her voice was light, almost musical, and instantly disarming.

He took that as an invitation to approach and drew up to the water's edge. "I can help with that."

"Be about it, then, Starkad."

THEY TOOK the night meal of boiled fish, and Starkad thought it the best he'd eaten in moons or more. And they talked long.

She spoke but a little of herself, saying she lived out here alone to avoid being taken by dvergar as a slave. Starkad could see why she'd fear it ... dvergar took women, especially those of such ethereal beauty. No one ever saw such slaves again. Some even claimed the dvergar ate them once they were finished using them for their perverse ends. Other tales told they planted their seed in women's bellies not so unlike trolls, and perhaps, like trolls, the birthing killed the hapless victims.

If Ogn knew aught of that, she did not say so.

Indeed, somehow, she convinced Starkad to speak of his own past, which had never been his wont before. But as the hour passed midnight, he told her how he'd come to Agder. And how Vikar had died. And he told her of the shadows haunting his dreams.

Maybe, he wanted anyone to confess his crimes to.

Maybe, he thought saying it aloud would somehow lessen the burden on his wretched heart.

And maybe it did.

Ogn had no mead or ale, but she offered him a skin of water, and he took it. "I don't know what your dreams mean, Starkad. Not for certain ... but I have heard tales. Perhaps this Odin drew power from Svartalfheim."

The very name sent shivers upon Starkad and made his hair stand on end. "Svartalfheim ..."

"The World of Dark. The shadows you described might have been mere fancy of your own fevered mind ..."

"Or perhaps svartalfar?" Starkad had heard but few tales of the dark alfar, none of them pleasant.

Ogn sipped her water, then murmured something under her breath. "We should sleep."

"I ... have no wish to sleep." Ever again.

"But you must. I will kindle the fire high as I can ... and will be here, close at hand. Should you cry out, I will wake you."

Except, in his nightmares, he could neither speak nor scream.

And still, what choice did he have? Sleep would come for him, sooner or later.

It always did.

PART III

Fifth Moon
Year 28, Age of the Aesir

19

The long walk back to Upsal gave Hervor more time to practice fighting with her left hand. Time enough to learn ... she'd sooner have managed to wrestle a troll than master this. Oh, Starkad taught her well, true enough, but a lifetime of practice with her right hand could not be simply transferred.

It was worse than starting over, even. Her every swing seemed off-balance. Clumsy.

And as for Starkad ... well, he lived, and that was a blessing. But he lacked the vigor she'd come to expect in him. After a day of walking and an evening of training, he'd collapse. Pale and sickly. Hardly the invincible man she'd known. Whatever this eitr was, his contact with it had drained him.

They came at last to Haki's hall where the thegns welcomed them back with grim expressions and shakes of their heads.

Hervor found Haki outside the hall, thrashing one of his men with the blunt of his sword. The poor sod had dropped his own axe and was lying in the muddy snow, unable to rise or fend off the beating.

"What was his crime?" Starkad asked one of the thegns.

"Naught at all. The king wished to fight and demanded Bjarke oblige. The king won." The thegn shrugged.

Oh. Hervor could not remember ever seeing Haki in such a foul mood. For a bare instant, she considered slipping off inside, unnoticed. She could grab the drinking horn, maybe find something left over from the day meal. But then again ... "My king?"

Haki spat, then spun on her. "Hervard!" He tossed his sword aside, heaved a few deep breaths. "Where the fuck have you been?"

"Seeking ... treasure, my king."

Haki spit again, then wiped sweat from his face. "So was Hagbard. And now he's fucking dead."

"Your brother?"

"Of course my godsdamned brother! You think I'd be so vexed over some *other* Hagbard? And now half my damned champions are off on their own, seeking *treasure*. I've a mind to sail to Skane myself and raze the whole fucking kingdom for this!"

Starkad grabbed her elbow. "I must seek out Wudga and prepare the eitr."

Oh, not now. "Please wait a bit. Allow me to deal with this ... situation."

"Hervor ... I am ... compelled to press on."

"Just *wait*." She looked back to Haki who now seemed half inclined to challenge another of his men. "My king. Might we speak alone?"

Haki grumbled something under his breath, then dunked his head into a barrel of water. He popped up an instant later, shivering and shaking his soaked hair about, splashing those nearby. Including Hervor. She backed away, saying naught. Finally, the king stormed off toward his hall, and Hervor followed.

The man grumbled every step of the way until at last settling down into his throne and fixing her with his glare.

"How did this happen?" Hervor asked.

"I do not have all the details, but the men say he was visiting the lands of Jarl Sigar."

"Sigar ... isn't he nephew to King Wolfsblood?"

"Same. Sigar has this daughter, Signe. Named after Wolfsblood's Hunalander wife, I think. Hagbard has fancied her a time now, and she had promised herself to him. So after we took the throne, he went to claim her. But some Hunalander challenged him for her hand. Hagbard killed him, his men, even one of Sigar's sons. And he thought the bitch loved him, thought himself safe. Our people told him not to go, so they claim. But he went to meet with Sigar, seek the man's forgiveness, pay the weregild and the bride price all at once."

Hervor groaned. It had obviously not gone according to Hagbard's plan.

"Bastard had him hanged."

Well, fuck. That sounded like war was the only answer. Unless ... "Supposing I convince Starkad and some of the others to accompany me. We kill Sigar and avenge Hagbard."

"Bah. What of Wolfsblood, then?"

"We don't even know if the king knew of or approved of his nephew's actions."

"Blood calls out for blood."

Oh, Hervor knew that all too well. Better than most. "If

you leave Upsal now, so soon after conquest, you risk losing your kingdom behind you. Besides, it is winter. Our ships are like to founder, and an army marched so far would be known long before it arrived."

"But you will succeed?"

"Starkad killed King Otwin not so long ago. Broke into his fortress and murdered him in the night. Let us go, and we'll see Sigar hanged from his own fortress. Then when summer comes ..."

"When summer comes, I'll fucking destroy all of Skane." Haki slammed his fist on the throne's armrest. "I'll hang that entire family. It'll be glorious, Hervor. Do you know the man betrayed and slaughtered the Volsungs of Hunaland? Think of the tales skalds will tell of the man who destroys that line."

She had heard as much, though it had happened many years back. With a nod, she fingered Tyrfing's hilt. "I will avenge Hagbard in your name, my king."

"I cannot say I well like leaving the task to someone else."

"This is why you have thegns and champions. You must rule your kingdoms or else risk losing them."

He waved her away, and she wandered the hall until someone was able to point her to Starkad. The man had already found the drink, settled into the nigh to empty feast hall beside a brazier.

Starkad looked to her as she approached but did not rise. "Word is, Wudga went to Dalar."

"To Gylfi's court?"

"Mmm. I'll have to go there in the morn. If you are still set on gaining some of the treasures of Glaesisvellir for yourself, you ought to accompany me."

She almost smiled at that. Finally, he seemed ready to acknowledge needing her help.

Shame she could not oblige. With a frustrated sigh, she slunk down on the bench beside him, then snatched the horn away and took a long swig. "Can't. I swore to avenge Hagbard on Sigar of Skane."

Starkad snorted. "You can barely fight anymore. You're not avenging anyone, woman."

"Yes." She sniffed. "That's why I told Haki you'd come with me."

"You fucking *what*?"

"I have to do this before I go hunting a runeblade, Starkad."

He glowered. "Well, I sure as the gates of Hel don't have to."

"Without you, I'm like to meet my end in Skane."

"Then you ought not to have offered!"

Hervor frowned. Despite his bluster, he wasn't going to actually let her go without him ... was he? Was it possible she had misjudged him? In trying to talk down Haki, she had volunteered Starkad without actually checking with him. And she seriously doubted she could do this without him.

"Look I ... Starkad. I'm asking you now for your help. Not for money, but for ... friendship."

He jerked the horn out of her hand, spilling mead all down her tunic. Hervor lurched backward at being so drenched. "You had no right."

"I saved you from that dragon."

"And I've saved your life more than once, I rather recall. Are we to track who owes who the most, now?"

He had a point. Damn him for it. She glowered at the man, then drummed her fingers on the table. "Do what you wish, Starkad. I go to Skane because my oath to Haki demands it." She rose and stomped away.

"Hervard!" Starkad shouted as she reached the door.

She paused, not turning back to him.

"I will look for you when I return from Dalar."

With a last shake of her head, she stormed out.

Damn him.

20

*N*aegling made short work of Ecgtheow's foes. The battlefield was littered with them, dead, or soon to be, dealt wounds that no armor protected against. The ancient runeblade gleamed in the failing daylight.

As Hrethel had predicted, King Haki had not expected an attack, least of all one coming from the marsh.

Jorund's loyal forces had stormed right up to Haki's wall, practically atop it before their foes even knew they were on them.

Now, the gates lay breached, most of Haki's thegns dead. Eikkr and his mercenaries had seen to that while Ecgtheow dealt with Haki's men outside the walls.

"Onward," Hrethel roared, pointing his sword at the open way before them.

He need not ask Ecgtheow twice. Naegling over his head, Ecgtheow charged forward, roaring for all he was worth.

"Remember, the king is mine," Jorund shouted from behind them.

Seemed unlikely to Ecgtheow. Eikkr was the stronger of

MATT LARKIN

the two brothers. Jorund would just get himself killed against a brutal warrior like Haki. Besides, if Eikkr didn't slay Haki, that was why Ecgtheow was here.

An axeman bleeding from a gaping wound above his brow barred Ecgtheow's way. Brave boy.

Ecgtheow grasped Naegling with both hands and brought the runeblade down in a mighty stroke. The warrior raised his axe to parry. Might have worked against a normal sword. Not Naegling, sharp and strong like no work of mankind. It sheared through the axe blade, the haft, and the wielder in a single stroke.

A quick shove sent the corpse out of his way, and then he was pressing on, through the gate.

Townsfolk ran screaming.

The whole place had descended into wild melees. To his left, a pair of men were dragging a woman into a stable by her hair. To the right, two shieldmaidens fought one another. And beyond, fires had sprung up here and there, workshops and houses ablaze, the flames lighting the town. Clogging it with thick smoke.

Ecgtheow cut down a woman who charged him, then Hrethel was at his side.

"Where is the king?"

Ecgtheow shrugged and spat. "Fled like a craven?"

Hrethel shook his head. "I think you do not know Haki ... there!" Again pointing with his sword.

Damn smoke obscured everything worse than mist. Ecgtheow had to squint to peer through it. Haki was engaged with Eikkr, blocking blows on his shield as Jorund's brother launched one furious attack after another.

Shit.

Ecgtheow charged forward. A flaming house collapsed

before him, spilling smoldering timbers in front of his path, forcing him to skid to a stop.

Hrethel drew up beside him. "Jorund said Haki was his."

"Jorund doesn't know what the fuck he's talking about. I aim to see him on a throne, not a pyre."

The jarl considered that a bare instant before nodding.

The pair of them ducked into an alley to bypass the burning wreckage. Around the next corner, Ecgtheow blundered to a stop again.

Before him, Eikkr had fallen to his knees, a great seeping wound carved out of his chest.

No man lived from such a blow.

"Haki!" Ecgtheow bellowed.

The Ostergotland king kicked Eikkr in the chest, sending him toppling into the mud before turning to look upon Ecgtheow.

Well then ...

"Protect Jorund," he said to Hrethel.

The jarl nodded.

Ecgtheow would handle the killing this day. He tromped over toward Haki, the other king meeting him halfway, staring up at him with fury in his eyes.

"Haki Seamaster," Ecgtheow said. "I consider this an honor."

"And you are?"

"Ecgtheow the Tiny."

Haki sneered. "One of those from that voyage to Thule."

So the king had heard of him. That was good. Good to know his fame had spread even to Ostergotland.

With a nod, Ecgtheow closed in. And then the king was on him, banging away with his sword. Ecgtheow blocked three blows with his shield, then shoved the king backward with it. His counterstroke might well have ended it right there had Haki not leapt back. Eyeing Naegling warily. He'd seen the gleam, seen the runes. Seemed to know what it meant.

"Another of the fell things, eh?" Haki hesitated a bare instant. Then he roared and charged forward with such ferocity Ecgtheow took a step back.

Man had killed Eikkr. He wasn't to be underestimated, then.

Ecgtheow blocked again and again, letting the king spend his fury. Around them, men screamed and died. A town burned. Ecgtheow had to keep his focus locked on his savage opponent. One misstep would prove his end.

The blows that rained down on his shield had begun to numb his arm.

But then, Haki's chest was heaving. Had to be nigh to breaking. The king swept his sword down again. This time, Ecgtheow raised his shield but jerked it away at the last moment, twisting his body out of the blade's path. Haki overextended, and Ecgtheow slashed him across the gut.

A shallow cut. Wouldn't have even pierced the mail ... had Ecgtheow carried a normal blade.

Haki fell back, glanced down at his stomach. Blood was oozing out from a gap in the mail. The king let a hand fall to his abdomen.

"You're dead now," Ecgtheow said.

Haki spit. Glared. "So it appears." He backed away a few steps, some hidden battle warring across his face. The grimace of pain, then. The wound must be spreading, festering. "I've a request then ..."

Ecgtheow shrugged. "Depends what it is, I suppose."

"Let the pyre be set upon one of my longships. I ... am a man of the sea."

And he wished to die out there. Ecgtheow could well see that.

Footfalls came up behind Ecgtheow, and he spun, Naegling raised. Hrethel and Jorund.

"I will grant your request, King Haki," Jorund said. "You slew my traitorous cousin, after all."

Haki nodded. And he sunk to his knees, clutching his guts.

THE SUN HAD SET NOW, and great bonfires lined the shores. Jorund's whole host had come up to Upsal, taken the town. Now men from both sides came to watch the grand funeral of the great sea king. No more fighting this day.

No, Haki had earned respect from all men of the North Realms, Ecgtheow supposed.

The king was nigh to dead when they laid him on the ship and shoved it off, into the sea. Jorund's men had laden that ship with kindling.

Now, as it drifted out, Ecgtheow held a piece of flaming tar-wood, standing in the lapping, freezing waves.

It fell to him, for he'd been the one to slay King Haki. He flung it, and it spun end over end through the darkness and landed atop the kindling. A good throw.

For a while, he watched the flames spread. They ignited the pyre upon which Haki laid—Ecgtheow could have sworn a mighty groan escaped the king, though no screams of agony. He would not have suffered long in any event. The flames leapt up and spread to the sails.

The burning vessel drifted farther and farther away, slowly vanishing into the mist.

Behind him, a skald had begun to recite an ode to the

fallen sea king, calling him beloved of Rán. Maybe he was, though the mermaid goddess hadn't saved him in the end. Still, he'd died brave. Maybe Odin awaited him in Valhalla.

Ecgtheow trod up to stand by Jarl Hrethel, who offered him a nod. The man was with his wife Gull and his daughter, a pretty young girl, maybe fourteen winters.

"Well then," Hrethel said, staring at the spot where the ship had disappeared. "I promised you land and wealth should we win this. Thanks to you, we have."

Ecgtheow nodded, too watching the funeral, half listening to the skald's words. Bitter and glorious and as expected—now talking of valkyries. "He fought well."

"As did you. My lands are south of here, nigh to the border of Njarar. Any number of islands nearby you can have your pick of."

"Islands? You promised me fields."

"Yes. Many of them have fields for growing crops. But if you find no island to your liking, we can come to another arrangement."

Ecgtheow nodded again. As long as Hrethel upheld his promise, he supposed it would do. "Your daughter ..."

"Ylva?"

"Is she a woman yet?"

The girl scoffed. "I surely am. And I can speak for myself!"

Ecgtheow chuckled. The girl had fire. He liked that.

Hrethel grunted. "You are a bold one, Tiny."

Now Ecgtheow turned to look at the jarl. A jarl's daughter was the best match he could ever dream of. In fact, many jarls might cut his throat for such dreams. Not Hrethel, though, Ecgtheow suspected. "You advised me to find a bride. What say you, Ylva? Would you marry a thegn and own an island with me? Perhaps even more than one ..."

Gull sputtered as if shocked at his presumption, but then, Ecgtheow knew his own worth. He'd made Jorund a king, and if Hrethel did not consent, well, he might seek recompense from Jorund himself.

"Well, Ylva?" Hrethel asked.

His would-be bride snorted. "I suppose he'll do." A mischievous wink.

Yes, Ecgtheow rather liked her.

21

Only rarely had Starkad set foot in Dalar. In truth, he knew it for obstinance, refusing to work with Odin's voice in Sviarland, to even walk King Gylfi's halls. Still, part of Starkad blamed Odin for all that had transpired. Part of him needed to, as if he himself did not have enough guilt to weigh down three lifetimes.

Despite his reluctance, Gylfi's men welcomed him into the king's hall. The king himself sat graciously upon his shadowed throne in the great hall.

"Starkad Eightarms." Though his voice was warm, if Gylfi smiled, Starkad could not make it out beneath the veil shadows around the king's face. "I did not think to see you again so soon. Did you meet your friend? Did you already bring me the price?"

Starkad grimaced. Hardly. And that delayed oath rankled at him, niggled his mind every step. "Before I can, I require something from one I hear is in your court for the winter. The man Wudga. Is he here?"

Gylfi chuckled at some private joke, as if he knew more

of Wudga than other men. As if he knew more of all things than other men.

Maybe he did.

"I gave Volund's son his own house, outside the town, in the foothills to the west. Call upon him if you must, though I think he fancies his solitude. He rarely comes to the court."

Starkad nodded, then turned to go.

"Starkad," the king said. "Do you know what befell Upsal in your absence? My sources tell me of war."

He shrugged. Haki seemed always engaged in one war or another. First with the Ynglings, now with Skane. None of it was Starkad's problem, and his oath to Haki was already fulfilled—and repaid well. "I care naught for Haki's schemes or woes." All that mattered was getting that runeblade for Gylfi and fulfilling his oath.

"May Odin speed your steps, then."

With a snort, Starkad left the hall. He trekked perhaps half an hour up into the foothills until he spied a small cabin there. A wall surrounded it, snow-covered stone five feet high. Out here wasn't quite the wilds but close enough for a man to worry over wolves and other beasts. The worse things, the things that came with the mist ... well, the wall wasn't half high enough to keep those out.

Starkad slipped through the gate and into the yard beyond. The small field beside the house might have grown some hardier crops in summer. Now, only a few signs of planting broke through the snows. Wudga had shuttered all the windows in the house, everything closed up so tight it seemed as if not even a breeze might slip in, though a slight plume of smoke wafted out of the chimney.

Around the front, Starkad rapped on the door. It swung inward, unlocked.

In the back of the room, Wudga sat on the floor, legs

folded beneath him, almost engulfed in darkness that the smoldering fire in the hearth failed to illuminate. Even the line of sunlight from the open door didn't do much to drive out the shadows here.

"What are you doing here, lingering in the dark?"

"Shut the door." The man's hair now seemed as jet black as his father's, his skin the color of ash.

Starkad reluctantly closed the door, then strode over to stand before Wudga. He yanked the skin of eitr from his belt and held it out before the man. "I brought it."

Wudga clucked his tongue, then stood, snatching the skin from Starkad's grasp. "And you shall have what I promised. Go ... take the cauldron from the hearth and dump its contents outside. I have another use for it at the moment."

Fine. Starkad made his way to the small fire. Inside the cauldron simmered the last dregs of a stew—deer by the smell of it. Rather than dump it, Starkad ladled it into a nearby bowl and then stalked over to a corner to eat.

As he did so, Wudga began to rummage through the house, gathering up other ingredients. If Starkad had not known better, he'd have sworn the man intended to start up another stew. No, but Wudga must now brew something darker and no doubt much less tasty if he was to fulfill his promise to Starkad.

The man soon slit his palm, squeezing drops of blood into the cauldron.

Starkad grimaced. He expected him to drink blood?

A good swig of the eitr followed, then powders Starkad dared to hope were spices. Perhaps Wudga wanted to make the taste palatable. Perhaps, though unlikely.

This seemed like to take a while, though, so Starkad shut his eyes.

🖋

He started awake, to find Wudga standing over him.

Starkad's fists were clenched. Vikar again. Always visiting him when he slept.

Wudga knelt beside him, offering him a drinking horn that sloshed with a dark liquid. Almost black, in fact.

With a groan, Starkad took the proffered horn. The stuff inside smelled of summer rains and dead men all mixed up together. A combination that turned his gut.

"Drink."

Eh. How badly did he truly desire this runeblade?

A nice thought, of course, but Starkad knew the truth. Even if he could have abandoned the prize for himself—and he knew he never would have—he could not break his oath to Gylfi. The man had saved Hervor, and Starkad had given his word. And if this was the only way …

He threw back the horn and drank. The fluid tasted worse than it smelled, so bitter he almost gagged. And thick, much thicker than water, like runny mucus. Choking, coughing, Starkad sputtered, spit some of it out.

"Drink it all."

The room had begun to sway like a ship at sea. Those shadows playing about. Singing. Hissing. Whispering.

Starkad had seen this sort of thing before.

"Drink it, Starkad. Your course is set. Falter now and I cannot say what would befall you …"

Again, he threw back the horn. Downed the rest of the vile concoction.

Let it fall from his hand and clatter to the floor.

His stomach heaved. It clenched and writhed until he pitched over sideways, clutching his gut and moaning.

And still the shadows danced.

*

They played for him, singing a chorus of darkness. Of madness claiming the minds of men and turning them away from their illusions of control, of light, of hope.

In the end, only chaos remained.

And all lights faded.

Starkad crawled through the pitch black, and voices laughed at him. Their sounds were alien, inhuman cackles that sent every hair on his body standing on end. His brain rejected the cacophony as impossible.

Beyond the world lay the fathomless dark.

And worse still, that darkness was not … quite … empty.

It watched him. Waited for him.

Odin had let it into Starkad's heart, and it knew him now. Knew him well, and demanded his obedience. Demanded he slowly damn himself, one great crime after another.

In the pale flicker of light, he saw Hervor running through deep woods, those too drenched in heavy shadows. She fled, panting, casting fevered glances over her shoulder as something chased her.

Her terror beat against his skull until his head seemed apt to burst. Whatever pursued her was gaining, growing closer and closer.

She was in danger.

She was going to … to die.

And he had let her walk into this.

One more death on his conscience. One more of his victims. Not of action, this time, but of inaction. Another woman he'd failed.

Grunting, he tried to push himself up. His stomach twisted itself in knots, and he heaved. Tried to wretch out all he'd drunk. Bile scorched his throat but the viscous fluid would not flow upward. It had seized his guts like a leech, latched on and lurching about inside him.

Had Wudga been wrong?

Or ... had he ... betrayed Starkad?

At the thought, the tiny flicker of light shifted, revealed the man, who had snatched up the skin of eitr. Wudga shook his head and clucked his tongue in dismay. And flashed a toothy smile.

Oh, the darkness did not encroach upon Wudga as it did on Starkad, as it had upon Hervor. No, it bent around Volund's son, as it had bent around Volund himself.

It became him, and he it.

Wudga had betrayed him ... though perhaps not in the way Starkad had first thought.

The eitr may have awakened the Sight in him ... but Wudga intended most of it for some other purpose.

Not that it mattered.

Naught mattered. Hervor was going to die.

And Starkad could not even stand.

22

Twenty-Two Years Ago

A day became many days with Ogn and then a fortnight. Until Starkad dared to dream of making her his wife. But she, who hid from dvergar for fear of slavery and lived with next to naught ... what had he to offer her?

And so he had set out to raiding, earning nigh to as much wealth as he had once enjoyed at Vikar's side.

And after long moons, he returned.

No plume of smoke rose from her cabin, though.

Starkad crept closer. The door lay open ...

"Ogn?" He turned about. Had the dvergar come for her after all? Had he left her alone only to fall to the slavery she so feared? "Ogn!"

Inside the cabin, everything seemed in its place. No sign of struggle. No fight ... her axe still lay on a shelf by the door. Had they caught her by surprise?

"Damn it," he mumbled. "Damn it. Ogn."

If those dvergar had taken her ... fuck. But he'd burn

down the halls of Nidavellir if he had to. He would get her back, no matter what.

And he had learned the woodsman's arts with Hermod himself, son of the great Agilaz. Trying to stay calm—you needed focus to track—he returned outside and glanced up at the sky.

Afternoon. A few hours of daylight before the sun set. Nights were longer this far north, especially in winter. It meant he didn't have much time.

He skirted about the edge of the cabin, watchful for any sign of ... there. A pair of tracks. One light, slender—Ogn clearly. And the other deep and large, a man who must be over seven feet tall. Surely no dverg, then. So what in the gates of Hel ... ?

A troll?

But would not a troll have carried her off over its shoulder? And smashed everything in the cabin while it was at it?

So a giant of a man had convinced her to come along, forced her, no doubt. Perhaps, knowing she could not win, she had not fought. Perhaps she dared to dream Starkad might return for her and keep his promise, wed her, and give her a better life.

Well, he would.

Trotting as fast as he could while following the trail, he raced from the valley.

He was coming for his woman. Ogn was the light he sought, the hope of his redemption. He needed her.

And he would not abandon her when she needed him.

THE TRAIL LED up to a mountain peak. Starkad pushed as hard as he could, but still the sun dipped below the horizon and a bitter wind whipped the snows and mist about his face. There was no tracking aught in such conditions.

Reluctantly, he pulled up short and hunted for an overhang or rock pile from which to take shelter. He found naught. And wandering in the dark was like to get him killed. One misplaced foot and he'd plummet off the side of the mountain and straight into some gorge.

Damn it.

Left with no other choice, he wrapped cloak and blanket both about his shoulders and settled down into the snows. He'd never get a fire going, so he'd have to rely on torches to keep the mist—and the worst of the cold—at bay.

It would be a long night.

છે.

THE FIRST RAYS of dawn broke through the mist, searing Starkad awake.

The dreams had been worse this night, though he'd once thought them better when Ogn was nigh. Perhaps he had lost her trail. Perhaps his mind punished him for losing her.

Muscles aching, he rose. His back cracked, his neck creaked. A thick layer of rime had crusted over his blankets and broke away as he stood.

Starkad sucked down a bitter, painful breath of the chilled air.

The torch must have burned out as he slept. Lucky mist-madness or deathchill hadn't taken him. He groaned, dug out another torch, and fumbled to light it with frozen fingers. The flint tumbled out of his numb grasp.

"Damn it."

He snatched up the thing and struck the steel a few

more times before managing a spark to light the torch. The oil-soaked rag flared to life a moment later. Starkad sniffed and rubbed his face. His cheeks burned with the cold, even beneath his beard.

Caught out overnight on a slope of Nidavellir, most men would have died. Well, Starkad was not most men. And he was going to get his woman back.

The wind and snows had half-buried the tracks. Now, he had to move more slowly. Deliberately. He couldn't lose the tracks ... nor could he afford to lose the daylight.

Another night like the last did not much appeal, assuming he managed to live through it again at all.

A long time he wandered the mountain, twice having to double back to find the tracks.

Around the edge of the next slope, a frozen waterfall plummeted into a gorge. Beautiful and glittering through the mist. Beyond it, barely visible beneath the layers of snow and the thick covering of mist, rose a rugged fortress. A dverg outpost?

Torch in hand, Starkad made his way past the falls and down to the fortress. It was blocky, as he imagined dverg design must be, but large. Rimmed by a parapet that had crumbled at one corner. Ice crusted over the better part of it, running down the parapet and beyond, halfway to where the snowdrift buried the foundations. The whole thing had been carved from blocks larger on a side than Starkad was tall.

Well, damn. This place seemed like something drawn from Niflheim, not a dverg ruin at all. To the side, only half visible from here, it seemed a portcullis sealed the main entrance.

As he drew nigh, the gate creaked, drawn up into the recesses of the fortress.

Well then.

Starkad planted the torch in the snow and drew both swords. And waited.

A man trod around the corner ... only it was not a man. It stood over seven feet tall, with sharp, angular features. Rugged muscles. And too much scraggly hair. Was that ... a jotunn?

Starkad balked, struggling not to back away. Tyr claimed to have fought one of these legendary creatures, but still, Starkad had doubted him. They were supposed to be banished beyond the Midgard Wall, into Jotunheim. And here, now, one strode toward him.

"What ... do you wish here, little man?" The jotunn spoke in accented Northern, its voice like rocks grating on one another.

"Where is Ogn?"

The jotunn glanced back at the fortress.

And there she was, standing upon the parapets, watching. This *thing's* prisoner ...

Well, Hel could have the jotunn, then.

"Jotunn. I challenge you to a holmgang for the woman."

"Starkad!" Ogn shouted from above. "Do not do this! Hergrimr will kill you!"

Oh, but it was already done. And he was not leaving here without her.

The jotunn slowly shook his head. "Human ... you are a fool."

"And you are a craven!" Starkad spat back.

Now the jotunn snarled. "Then I accept. And we shall fight at the falls below, at dusk."

Starkad nodded.

Let it be done.

23

A small party had the best chance of sneaking into Sigar's fortress, killing him, and escaping undetected. Not so unlike what they'd done in Njarar. Save that, back then, Hervor had had Starkad beside her. Well, now she had Folke and Kare, champions of Haki like herself. Plus a pair of shieldmaidens she trusted, Gyda and Inkeri.

She'd even revealed her true gender to them all. It was too hard to conceal it now, over the long trek. Especially with one arm only half working.

Folke had looked at her with dumb shock on his face.

Kare had asked her to lay with him.

And the shieldmaidens ... they were harder to read, at first. Later though, on the road, Gyda had said she wished she'd tried it, hiding her sex. Hervor didn't much know what to tell the woman.

And now here they were in the marshlands of Skane, the five of them, all sneaking about. It was almost like her days as a bandit with Red-Eye's Boys, save that these men and women had a hint more honor. Or they'd have called it that ... they'd only raze and pillage and rape the villages their king called enemy. But to the villagers, Hervor imagined it all seemed about the same, bandit or raider.

And she had reason not to dwell on any of it.

Sigar was an imbecile to have executed Hagbard, no matter what the man had done. Whatever befell the people here, the blame for it lay at their jarl's feet. So then.

"So all those days we were raiding," Folke said. "Back then, right?"

Hervor glanced at him. "Yes?"

"And when we sacked Upsal and killed Ochilaik ... you were a woman then too?"

Hervor faltered in her steps, exchanged a look of bewilderment with Gyda. "Yes, Folke. More-or-less have been a woman since birth."

Gyda snickered. "Usually how it works, my friend."

They pushed lightly through the woods, drawing ever closer to the fortress. Beyond the wood's edge, the fortress came into view. The jarl didn't have his warriors patrolling, but he did have a few watching the town, protecting it from raiders or aught else. And his fortress, well, of course, that had a watch up on the wooden palisade surrounding it.

"So you ... you never had a cock."

Now Gyda sputtered with laughter.

When she could finally keep a straight face, Hervor looked to Folke. "As it happens, I've had several. I just didn't keep any of them."

He balked. "W-why not?"

"Their owners were attached to them."

Now all the others snickered, and Inkeri slapped Folke on the back of the head. "Looking to fasten the name Rockhead, are you?"

"Folke Rockhead," Hervor said. "I like it."

"Folke Rockhead," Kare repeated. "The man who needed it explained that women don't have cocks."

Hervor raised a hand to quiet them. "Fall back to that clearing we saw a bit ago. I don't want your mockery to alert the men up there."

"How do you plan to get inside?" Gyda asked.

"We wait for nightfall."

She had until then to come up with a plan.

§

MUCH AS HERVOR had despised climbing up to Otwin's castle in the dark, the strategy had worked in Njarar and she saw no reason it could not work now. If they could find a section of the fortress not well patrolled, they might grapple over the side, climb the wall, and be inside before anyone knew they had come.

If all went well.

As the sun dipped below the horizon, she rose. Best get this done.

"We don't know just how many men Sigar has in there with him," she said. "So don't be seen until we have no choice. Kill those you must, but keep it quiet."

Easy advice to give. Harder to follow.

All her practice at fighting left-handed had gotten her back up to the level of a boy handling a real sword for the first time. If Sigar was protected by children, she'd stand a chance. So long as there weren't too many of the little bastards.

"Who should lead the assault?" Gyda asked.

Odin's balls. That ought to have fallen to Hervor. Easy. She'd earned it a dozen times over. But now ... now she'd only get them all discovered. Then killed. Dying like a fool was not like to impress the Aesir, now was it?

"Kare will lead." The man was slightly less brawny than Folke, perhaps, but he had at least half a brain. That counted for more on this kind of mission.

Kare nodded grimly, then turned to go.

A wolf's howl welcomed in the rising moon. Another answered it. And another. A chorus of howls that just did not stop.

"What in the gates of Hel?" Gyda said.

"Sounds like wolves," Folke offered.

A lot of wolves, very close. Closer than they ought to have drawn to a group of humans. She exchanged a look with Gyda.

"There's tales," the shieldmaiden said. "Stories of varulfur in the woods of Skane."

"Varulfur?" Kare said. "This close to a village?"

So then. Press the attack and risk being harried by wolves—of one kind or another—while trying to sneak or draw them off? Only one choice really made sense.

"Weapons." Hervor reached to pull Tyrfing off her shoulder then stumbled as a spasm wracked her neck and arm. Couldn't get her arm that high. All that practicing wielding the blade left-handed, but she'd slung it over the wrong shoulder out of habit. A habit she'd have to break.

Besides, she ought to know better than to draw until a foe was in sight. The blade had taught her that lesson long ago.

"Move," she snapped. "Move back, deeper into the wood —we cannot risk discovery. Quickly!"

Kare led the way, darting amongst the trees so skillfully Hervor had trouble even tracking him. The others fell in behind him, pushing hard.

Her ankle snared on the snow-buried root. Twisted. Sent her colliding into a tree trunk.

A dusting of snow poured down overtop her. Gyda grabbed her elbow and yanked her around the tree. It had rapidly grown dark, and they'd had no torches out. Had planned to sneak up to the fortress.

Fucking mist was everywhere. Couldn't see a damned thing.

A heavy form tromped through snow in the darkness behind her. Underbrush rustled off to her left.

Hervor pushed Gyda forward, then chased after her.

Where was it? Something was definitely after them.

Snarls and snaps rang out from all sides.

Folke pulled up short, mighty sword grasped with both hands. "Go!" he bellowed. "There's rocks up ahead. High ground. Get up the—"

A mass of black fur and snarls flew through the air and collided with Folke. The pair of them vanished into the mist.

"Rockhead!" Gyda screamed.

Hervor now did jerk Tyrfing free. Its fiery light reflected off the mist and stung her eyes, not increasing her vision by much. "Come to me and die!"

Another flying form slammed into Gyda just to Hervor's side. The wolf bore the shieldmaiden down and crashed into the snow, throwing up a dusting of it. Gyda shrieked and wrestled with the beast as Hervor raced over.

Bellowing her rage, Hervor thrust Tyrfing into the wolf's hide. The blade bit deep, split flesh with ease. The wolf yelped, spun with startling agility and launched itself at Hervor. Its weight yanked her blade from her hand and sent her tumbling backward.

The creature landed atop her. Huge. Heavy as a fucking troll.

Its eyes gleamed with fell light. Its jaws snapped at her face. Hervor screamed, pushed away at it with her good arm. Tried to raise her right arm to hold it back. A haze of pain blurred her vision, even through the rush of battle rage that had seized her.

Hot saliva dripped into her eyes as the varulf snapped and snapped.

Another weight slammed down atop it. In the darkness, Hervor couldn't see shit. Blood squirted out of the varulf. It leapt off her, flinging Gyda to the ground. The shieldmaiden pitched over to her side, hand clutched around Tyrfing's hilt.

The varulf stalked around them. Gaze darting back and forth between its prey and the mist. Great gouges marred the beast. Wounds that would have slain man or wolf ... removing any doubt that this creature was a fell mergence of both.

But then, Tyrfing would claim even this monster. It just didn't know the poison had already seeped inside it.

Beside Hervor, Gyda gasped and spurted. She turned to the shieldmaiden. The woman gurgled up blood and fell to her knees. The wolf had torn open a ragged wound between Gyda's shoulder and neck. Fangs had sunk into her chest, her arm. Blood was gushing from these wounds.

Fuck.

When Hervor looked back, the wolf had vanished into the mist.

Gods damn it!

She raced over to Gyda's side and flung the shieldmaiden's arm around her good shoulder. It meant holding Tyrfing with her right hand—which meant she couldn't raise it above the height of her chest. But it was that or abandon the woman.

Who was already fucking dead, from wounds like that.

More screams rang out in the night.

"Kare!" Hervor bellowed.

"Over here," the voice answered after a moment.

She followed the sound of it, racing in the dark. Tyrfing's faint light was all she had to keep her from colliding with a tree or tripping over another godsdamned root. Her ankle still pained her from the first. Made carrying Gyda even more difficult.

"Come on, woman," Hervor muttered. "Come on."

No answer.

And the sudden stink of shit.

Gyda's foot snared on something, and she did naught to aid Hervor in carrying her. They both tumbled to the ground.

No.

No ...

Hervor rolled the other woman over. Her eyes stared up, empty. The blood had stopped pumping from her numerous wounds.

"I ..." Hervor panted. "I'm sorry." She scrambled up. Had to keep moving.

Had to get back to Kare and hope he'd managed that high ground. Otherwise, none of them would last the night.

24

*Y*lva wore a crown of flowers in her hair, looking fresh as summer dew, like a creature stepped out of Alfheim. Even were she not the daughter of a jarl and thus a mighty step forward for Ecgtheow, he'd have been pleased by the match. Such a woman was like to give him strong sons and daughters, enough to make a good life for himself.

She stood on a rise just before the woodlands, above the gathered crowd, winking mischievously at him as he drew nigh. Indeed, she seemed well pleased enough with the match. Ecgtheow had always said get yourself a happy wife, or you were like to find more peace beyond the gates of Hel.

Ecgtheow returned her smile as he joined her atop that hillock. He'd already traded the bride price for the dowry, and Hrethel seemed well enough pleased, though Ecgtheow could never have made it an even trade with a jarl.

But a pleased father-in-law ... that too boded well.

Ecgtheow had to blink in the afternoon light, reflecting off the mist. The day was bright, and someone claimed

Sunna was smiling on the wedding, though Gylfi's people had told men to stop invoking the Vanir for years now.

Way Ecgtheow saw it, better to have too many gods than not enough. Aesir, Vanir—new gods, old—let them all be pleased.

Shame his own father couldn't have been here for this, though. Valkyries had come for him long winters ago ... but at least Hrethel was there, nodding his approval, his wife looking more solemn by his side.

The crowd parted as an elderly woman made her way toward the hillock, blue and red paint marking her face, hair tied in wild braids. She leaned heavily on a walking stick during the climb, a wand perhaps ... Ecgtheow heard the witches used wands in their Art or pretended to.

The völva's face was almost as grim as Gull's. Perhaps the woman had actually cared about Haki who had ruled here so recently. Still, a völva had to serve the lord of a kingdom, whoever he may be. Now, it was Jorund.

He flinched when the witch pointed that stick at him.

Slowly, she turned to Ylva, pointed it at her too.

Now the bride squirmed, looking almost as uncomfortable as Ecgtheow felt.

Then the old völva banged the wand on the ground thrice and began to speak in old verse, accented in ways his distant ancestors might have spoken. Then again, who knew how men spoke during the Old Kingdoms? No one lived to say it.

It went on for long enough he found himself fighting to hold still. Just had to focus on the girl's face, all grins and nervousness.

"In the name of the goddess Frigg, do you accept this woman?"

"Yes." His voice sounded scratchy in his own ears.

"And you, Ylva, in Frigg's name, will you have this man as your husband?"

"Yes."

The völva slammed her wand onto the ground again. "Then bring forth the sacrifice!"

One of Hrethel's men led a goat toward the völva by a rope around its neck, the animal placid and having no idea what urd now lay before it. The beast was healthy, large enough to make up the better part of tonight's feast. It had formed a large part of the bride price he'd paid to Hrethel, after all, so he'd bought the best he'd found in all Upsal.

The völva laid a bowl beneath the goat and looked to Ecgtheow. He grabbed the animal by the horns to hold it in place. At once, it began to thrash and struggle. It may not have known what was coming, but it did not like being so manhandled. With a swift and well-practiced motion, the völva drew a knife across the animal's throat.

In a few heartbeats, all fight went out of the goat, and it sank to its knees, slowly bleeding out while the völva invoked Frigg and other goddesses of fertility. Through her mumbling, it was hard to say, but Ecgtheow would have sworn she mentioned the name Freyja under her breath, another of the cast-down Vanir. Some ways died hard, and the witch was old enough to remember, to have worshipped the Vanir half her life.

When the goat grew still, the völva dipped two fingers into the bowl of blood and traced a thin line of it along Ecgtheow's forehead. Then she repeated the gesture on Ylva. The witch then flicked droplets of blood over the nearest guests, blessing them all with Frigg's bounty.

"Now the sword," the völva said.

With a grunt, he produced Naegling and offered it to

Ylva. "This blade is for our firstborn son to bear. No finer blade graces the face of Midgard."

Without taking her eyes from his face, Ylva belted the sword about her waist. Symbolic, of course. She'd return it to him until their son was old enough to need it.

Next, they traded rings and made their vows.

All so glorious.

Ecgtheow dared to hope Frigg truly did watch this and Odin too and Freyja for that matter. Maybe one of them would ensure him a happy marriage and many children.

Naught else mattered more, after all.

IN THE DAYS following the wedding feast, some of the guests had departed, but Jorund had welcomed a great many of his jarls, thegns, and their war bands to remain. And too, those of Haki's own former people who would swear oaths of loyalty, he took into his service and welcomed to his table.

No man passed on free food and mead, Ecgtheow supposed.

In the new king's hall, Ylva sat with her father, speaking softly, while Ecgtheow milled about and eyed the other warriors. Not a fortnight ago, some of these men had been enemies. Now, Jorund insisted they all become one kingdom.

Ecgtheow would do as the king commanded, of course ... and being now tied to Hrethel, Jorund was maybe more his king than Gylfi. Strange thought, that.

Either way, it was hard not to mistrust those who had tried to kill you. Ecgtheow would just as soon be off to the island Hrethel had promised to him and Ylva. As soon as winter broke, they'd be planting the fields in the hopes of a good crop before the summer passed.

Besides, if he hadn't already planted a son in Ylva, he aimed to keep trying.

The thought brought a grin to his face.

As Ecgtheow claimed the drinking horn from a house-carl, Jorund rose from his throne in the back of the room.

The king himself, they saw less and less of in the past days. He came out in the evening for the feasts but sat alone on his throne, shadowed and reclusive, much as Gylfi had been. But Gylfi was old and perhaps even a sorcerer and had his excuses for his unmanly and unsociable behavior. Jorund … seemed a different man than he had been a moon ago.

Now, slowly, everyone turned to see what he'd say. Last he'd spoken at all had been his order to welcome those of Haki's people who'd swear to him. So what now?

The king stalked forward, eerily silent, and paused several feet before one of the great braziers lighting the feast hall. "My fellows." His voice did not boom, nor sound shouted, and yet it seemed to echo from every corner of the room. "We have victory now—Upsal is ours."

A cheer went up, men raising drinking horns, toasting their victory, as if they had not done that oft enough in the past days.

"Such a force as ours has not been assembled in count-less winters."

Another cheer, and Ecgtheow had to join in. After all, not long ago, men would have called Haki unassailable. They truly did have a fine army here.

"So then," Jorund said when the shouting had died down. "Why must we stop here? Haki spoke of a united

Sviarland, but the glorified pirate had neither the wit nor the stones to achieve this. We, my fellows, have both."

Now, fewer men cheered. Others murmured in confusion. Ecgtheow folded his arms across his chest. What *was* Jorund on about now? Ecgtheow had once dreamed of uniting the land under Gylfi ... was that Jorund's plan?

"Ostergotland has no king, and thus, that must be our first target."

Oh. Well, that posed a difficulty. If Jorund claimed Upsal and Ostergotland, it left Olof Sharpsighted's new claimed kingdom of Njarar surrounded by Jorund's lands. How long before Jorund decided to claim Njarar as well, at the expense of Gylfi's former thegn? The king of Dalar would not like that overmuch, Ecgtheow felt certain.

"Now is the time to strike," Jorund said, "before anyone can suspect it. Men do not make war in winter, they say. The nights are too long, too cold. The seas treacherous ... but we can strike by land and sea, for we fear naught. And only one kingdom truly stands in the way of uniting all Sviarland."

Ecgtheow groaned. Fuck.

"Old King Gylfi of Dalar has had his day. And now, we will go to him and ask him to swear his loyalty to our new realm."

Slowly, Ecgtheow shook his head. It didn't seem urd was like to let him plant a damned thing in the near future. And his island would have to wait ... maybe for quite some time.

25

With the silver Haki had paid him, Starkad had purchased the fastest dogs he could and pushed them so hard one had died on the third day. Such brutality chafed him. The animals deserved better.

Still, he'd had no choice but to stop, buy more dogs, and press on.

And in stopping, he'd heard the news spreading from Upsal. Haki murdered by the sons of Yngvi, this Jorund now on the throne. No king of Upsal seemed to reign long these days. All war and blood ... and Starkad had no idea how to feel about any of it.

He'd been loyal to Jorund's grandfather, true, but that was long winters past.

And the only thing Starkad could think on these days was the danger he'd seen Hervor in. And so he pushed the dogs harder.

Until at last he came to a village in the domain of Jarl Sigar.

It was small, surrounded by a wall that might keep out wolves and bears, but would not stand overlong against a determined force of men. Inside the village, one of the jarl's thegns had set up an equally unimpressive hall but one into which he welcomed guests.

A good place to start asking after Hervor. She must have stopped somewhere for supplies. She must still be alive.

She must ...

"Starkad?" Her voice.

He spun to find her there. Fresh scratches on her face, bandages on her arm. By her stood another of Haki's champions, the man Kare, and with them, a shieldmaiden who looked even more beaten down than Hervor herself.

The urge to throw his arms about her took him, but he beat it down. After the way they'd parted ...

"I, uh ... I am glad you live."

She nodded, then waved for him to follow her to a table. "The jarl's men are generous enough ... when we offered them silver trinkets as presents."

And presumably did not reveal the purpose of their trek to Skane.

"So you did not try to ..."

She shook her head, then spoke of an attack by varulfur. Starkad grimaced at her tale. Was that what his ... vision ... had revealed? She was lucky to be alive at all. Not all of the party were that lucky. Folke had been a good man. A moron, but an honest one. Brave.

Starkad rubbed his head. Had he been here, had he gone with her when she asked ... was it part of his curse to always fail those around him? Or was that an excuse?

"Now you're here," Hervor said, "maybe we can finish this."

"I'd wager those varulfur serve Jarl Sigar."

The wounded shieldmaiden groaned.

Hervor just snorted. "You think a man commands those beasts?"

Why not? The Ás tribes had used varulfur and berserkir, both. Especially the Godwulf tribe. For certain the shifters proved dangerous, hard to control. They also provided unmatched ferocity in battle and unrivaled ability as scouts and trackers.

Starkad sighed. "If you truly wish it, we can pursue Hagbard's vengeance. But there is something else you should know before making that decision."

"What is it?"

"You remember the sons of Yngvi, whom Ochilaik warred with and finally drove away?"

She shrugged, then winced, obviously still pained by her numerous wounds. Perhaps her shoulder would *always* pain her, despite the bargain Starkad had made with Gylfi. "Cravens who abandoned their kingdom. What of them?"

"As soon as you were away from Upsal, these sons, Jorund and Eikkr, attacked. Haki is dead, and Jorund sits on the throne of Upsal."

Hervor's face grew darker and darker with each word he spoke, until, finally, she gave a slight shake of her head. "He … murdered my king."

"So the tales tell it."

Kare slapped the table. "Then we must avenge King Haki without delay."

"What of Sigar?" Hervor asked.

Kare shrugged. "For all we know, the man betrayed Hagbard to draw Haki's champions from his side. Either way, that vengeance may be left for Hagbard's own sons if need be. The longer we let Jorund sit on that throne, the more he'll consolidate his power. Come summer it may be too late to avenge Haki."

The other shieldmaiden cleared her throat. "I am ... in no shape to fight any war."

Nor did Hervor seem to be, from what Starkad could see.

He scratched his beard. "If I asked you to let all this go ... even asked you to come with me to Glaesisvellir ..."

"Fuck Glaesisvellir, Starkad. I beg you now, as your friend. Please help me avenge Haki. I ... cannot pay you much, but aught I have—save Tyrfing—it is yours."

Damn it.

He'd known that was coming.

And the last time he'd refused her, she'd tromped off on her own and come within a hair's breadth from rotting in the marsh.

So really, he had no choice.

This was why a man should not become too close to others. Especially not to women.

THEY RODE from Skane and into Ostergotland, and there the paths grew thick with refugees. Whole families trudging through the snows, bearing their bundled-up lives upon their backs.

There, a girl not more than five winters, bent almost double under the weight of a pack. Behind her, a grandmother heaving, trying to manage a bundle of wood. And in the front, the mother, panting but still standing, no doubt bearing the heaviest burden of all.

No sign of a husband, of a father to the girl.

And Starkad had seen dozens of families like them.

"Where are you bound?" he asked the woman.

"Skane. Hoping Siggeir Wolfsblood will take pity on us."

Starkad scratched his beard. Siggeir Wolfsblood was

known for having about as much pity as a troll. Starkad could give the woman a bit of wealth, but that would only prove an excuse for her neighbors to murder her. If not them, then the men she turned to for help.

"What's happened?" Hervor asked.

"King Jorund has invaded Ostergotland. Maybe Dalar, too, if rumors be true."

Hel.

So much for waiting for summer. Instead of gathering his forces and securing his throne … Jorund seemed to think he could simply kill every rival in Sviarland. But then, Ostergotland had just lost its king, as well. Jorund's plan seemed not so unlike Vikar's own, long winters back.

Starkad shook his head. "Pass straight through Skane and, if you can, take a boat on to Sjaelland. Healfdene's son Hrothgar rules Reidgotaland now and is far more like to offer succor than Siggeir Wolfsblood. Seek him out."

The woman nodded, clearly doubtful about her chances of making it across even a narrow stretch of the Gandvik Sea in winter. As doubtful, perhaps, as Starkad was.

"You know this Hrothgar?" Hervor asked when the family had moved on.

"Barely. He's a shadow of the king Healfdene was, but a good man, or so it seemed to me." Probably a better man than Starkad.

They pressed on until they came to another party on the road, this one not refugees but a small war band.

Starkad guided Hervor and the others off the road to let the war band pass—two dozen men here, no more. Except the big man leading them … that was Tiny—Ecgtheow.

The man looked in Starkad's direction, then called for a halt. He said something to a warrior beside him, then the pair of them trudged over.

"Tiny?" Hervor said.

He nodded at her, face solemn as a rock. "Hervor. Starkad. It's good we found you."

Starkad's fingers twitched. "Were you looking for us?"

"Yes."

"Who's your companion?"

"Starkad Eightarms, I present Jarl Hrethel of Upsal. My father-in-law."

The man's hair was streaked with gray, his scars speaking of more than one battle behind him. The jarl nodded.

"I congratulate you on your marriage, Ecgtheow." Starkad turned to the other man. "Hrethel ... one of the jarls who swore for Jorund, isn't it?"

Beside him, Starkad felt Hervor reach for her blade.

"I did."

"And you are looking for us ..." Starkad's own hands edged closer to his swords. He truly did not want to fight Ecgtheow, but if the man had cast his lot in with Jorund ...

Ecgtheow's gaze locked on Starkad's hands. "We may have all made poor choices in the past. I aim to set right what can be set right ... and avenge what cannot."

At the obvious tension, Hrethel's men had begun to draw nigh, hands on weapons. The anticipation of violence had already grown thick in the air, heady and apt to make men act without thought. Starkad knew it all so well.

"Meaning, what?" Hervor demanded. "I thought you a thegn to Gylfi."

"So I was," Ecgtheow said. "I do not know now even if he would take me back ... I came into Jorund's service and Hrethel's. But Jorund has changed much in very little time."

Starkad glanced at Kare and Inkeri, who too had hands

on weapons and had begun to flank Ecgtheow. "Changed how?"

Hrethel twitched, then spat. "Grown dark ... and over-bold. He threatens to turn even upon Gylfi, the king who so openly sheltered him."

Given the sorcery Gylfi wielded, Starkad wasn't sure he favored Jorund in such a conflict.

"It's worse than that," Ecgtheow said. "He's got draugar fighting for him, at least two dozen of them."

Hervor scoffed. "*Draugar?* You're shitting me, Tiny."

"The three of us know draugar only too well, shield-maiden. That and he has a new champion, a man some claim cannot be slain, cannot be defeated."

"Who?" Starkad demanded.

"They're calling him the Walking Kraken. Calling him invincible."

Starkad shook his head. "No one is invincible."

And Starkad had slain foes men might have thought such about.

26

Twenty-Two Years Ago

*H*ergrimr had allowed Starkad to place torches around their battleground and that light now reflected off the frozen falls, as Starkad danced around his foe. The jotunn carried a sword as long as Starkad was tall, with a blade wider than his thigh. A single swipe of that would have sheared through mail and flesh and bone. Would have chopped Starkad right in half.

Would have cut down a fucking tree.

And so Starkad leapt out of reach once again. He dodged. Feinted. Rolled under Hergrimr's mighty swings.

And the jotunn swung and swung, chest heaving with the effort of it. Despite the speed with which he could swing that monstrous sword, Hergrimr's recoveries were slow. And getting slower.

Another strike slammed down into the snow.

Starkad dodged to the side, darted in, and whipped his own blade around. It tore a shallow gash along Hergrimr's shin and sent the jotunn stumbling forward. Starkad pressed his edge and slashed along the jotunn's face, drawing a long, wicked gash there.

As Hergrimr roared, Starkad rolled off to the side, diving out of the way of another mighty cleave of that sword. Again, the jotunn charged in. Now blind with rage, with frustration. Clearly not used to facing a foe that could so evade his every move.

The fastest man was the only one who mattered.

Not even jotunn strength made up for it.

Starkad twisted away from another blow. Hergrimr overextended, and Starkad countered, Vikar's sword biting into the jotunn's elbow. That mighty sword tumbled down into the snow. The jotunn stared dumbly at his blood, gushing out over the snows.

Let him gape. It gave Starkad the chance to close inside the monster's reach. He whipped one blade around, opening Hergrimr's throat and rammed the other through the jotunn's gut.

The monster fell back, then pitched over, clutching its one good hand to its neck. Blood oozed out between those fingers. And the jotunn slumped down into the snow.

Panting himself, Starkad let his swords drop and bent over, hands on his knees. The cold stung his lungs. A single blow from that thing would have ended him, and all Odin's dark ritual would have meant naught.

Damn.

Snow crunched nearby, barely audible over his own gasping breath. Still, he looked up to see Ogn, ashen-faced, shaking her head.

"What have you done?"

"I ... saved you." He panted. He needed some water. He needed to sit down. "Now we can be wed."

"I was not yours to save ..." She knelt by the fallen jotunn and stroked his face with one hand.

What the fuck?

"Ogn?"

"Damn you, Starkad Eightarms. Damn you forever ..."

Now he truly saw her. Thick with child. So thick she must have conceived not long after he'd left ... if not before.

"W-what? I just fought for you ..."

Ogn rose, her fingers clasped around the hilt of Vikar's sword. "I didn't ask to be saved! You ... bastard ... you ..." She shook her head. "It was your brother's sword, yes? The one you betrayed? Slaughtered? Everywhere you go, you bring death ..."

Starkad straightened, slowly, hands up in warding. She stood between him and the other sword. No. No, he needed no blade, for she would never harm him.

"He was a good man ..." Tears had welled in her eyes. "We were, our child was ..."

"H-he kidnapped you!"

She frowned. "It ... might have started like that ... but you. You did not bother to ask ... you just came and brought death. As you always do. You bought your life with darkness. So may darkness take you, Starkad." She panted, as if barely able to hold back the weeping.

"I ... I love you, Ogn. Please, we can talk about this." He took a halting step toward her.

She hefted the sword, clearly not accustomed to it, but armed, nonetheless. "May darkness hold you, always. I damn you to it ... to never find peace. To always wander, never satisfied, never able to hold the wealth you claim."

"Ogn! Do not speak such things." Starkad edged toward her. He just had to wrest the sword away, then they could talk. She was disturbed, but surely they could work this out.

"May all your days be drenched in blood and bereft of joy."

He flinched at her use of Vikar's words from his nightmare.

"Death shall follow in your wake all your life, Starkad. And your crimes will overshadow even your fame."

Every word fell upon him like a blow. They swelled around his heart and crushed it, surely as the pressure he felt in his nightmares. They brought him to his knees.

And he crawled, begging for forgiveness. But as in the dreams, no words came.

Ogn backed away. And she turned Vikar's sword backward, toward her own breast.

Starkad opened his mouth. Tried to shout her name. The words choked him, refused to escape his throat.

With a last, hateful glare at him, Ogn flung herself down. Her weight, light though it was, proved more than enough. The sword punched through her gut and out her back.

And finally, the scream broke from Starkad's throat.

It echoed off the mountains. It sent snows tumbling down from the peak.

Anguish, despair, and insurmountable guilt mingled in his cry. But no one answered.

PART IV

Sixth Moon
Year 28, Age of the Aesir

27

Beneath a sheen of blood, Tyrfing gleamed in Hervor's left hand. She'd cut down men, and it had been the hardest battle of her life. Every movement was an unnatural struggle fighting like this. Her instincts defied her judgment. And she earned cuts and gouges aplenty across her face, her arms, and her legs.

But then again, she'd slain five of Jorund's men.

They fought not ten miles from Grandfather's lands now. No doubt his own soldiers fought nearby, as well.

They'd turned these hills into a charnel ground. The snows melted beneath hot blood and steaming guts and hundreds of dying men. And still, the brunt of Jorund's army came on, even as the sun dipped lower and lower. Like they didn't plan to take respite at night?

And why not, if Ecgtheow was right. If the draugar served Jorund, the moment the last rays of sunlight winked out, the dead would become her greatest foes. Enemies against which she could not possibly win now, given her useless arm.

She'd thought vengeance complete against the Ynglings.

And here, against all odds, against all reason, another Yngling had reclaimed the throne of Upsal. And did Hervor's ancestors now writhe in the Otherworld, cursing her and holding her oath unfulfilled?

Gasping, she snared a blade against her shield. Twisted away as her foe swung again and again.

Jarl Hrethel's shield slammed into Hervor's attacker and drove the bastard backward. Her foe slipped in the muck and toppled onto his arse. Hervor lunged forward, running Tyrfing right through the man's mail, his chest, and out his back.

Another one down.

On they fought, she and Hrethel and the jarl's men. Atop the hill, Kare had slaughtered enough foes to put Hervor to shame. Once, she might have been his match. Once. Now she was just grateful he was on her side.

And Starkad ... well, he had stormed through Jorund's troops like a whirlwind, leaving a wake of severed limbs and corpses as he passed, ever hunting the king. No doubt intent to put an end to this all.

Not so long ago, Hervor would have demanded that honor for herself. Would have thought only she could complete her vengeance against the Ynglings. But it might take moons more for her shoulder to finish healing ... if it ever did.

"Behind you!" Hrethel shouted.

Hervor spun, caught another blow on her shield, and engaged yet another soldier of the bastard Ynglings. Their army seemed never to end.

She cut this man down as well, then limped over to where one of Hrethel's men had fallen. Dead, an axe in his sternum.

Finally, the enemy line seemed to break. Jorund's men

fell back, giving Hervor a desperately needed respite. She slipped to her knees, panting. And as she wiped the blood and gore and sweat from her face, the sun set.

With it, her heart clenched. Not this again. Not this ... terror. This horror she'd thought she'd left far behind on Thule.

A sudden, uncontrollable panic settled over her. It squeezed her heart and closed her throat, suffocating her with the knowledge of what had to come next.

Not again ...

෨

HERVOR WATCHED, as a figure stalked about the hill. Coated in black mail that reflected no light and beneath it, a shroud pulled tight around his face. Kare turned on this approaching apparition.

Grunting, Hervor hefted Tyrfing to join them. But from the flanks came a shambling man, dragging a lamed leg behind it, along with an axe big enough to fell a tree in a single swipe. And those gleaming ... Hel-cursed ... red eyes.

She whimpered, then hoped no one had heard it. Not this again ...

Tyrfing up before her, Hervor advanced on the draug. For there was naught else she could do save fight or run.

And she wasn't about to run.

෨

HRETHEL'S BLADE bit down into the draug's back.

The creature faltered in its attack on Hervor. Gazed down at the sword point sticking out of its chest. And then it shrieked, the sound mind-grating, like winds escaping from the gates of Hel. It surged at her.

The jarl yanked on his blade, pulled it off balance.

Gave Hervor the chance she needed.

"Die, trollfucker!" She rammed Tyrfing through its face.

And finally, it fell still.

Four of their men had died to bring this thing down.

Hervor jerked her blade free, then turned back to the hill.

Kare was still engaged with the shrouded figure and clearly overmatched. It rained blow after relentless blow upon him, until finally his sword flew from his hands. Jorund's champion tried to back away, but his foe cleaved a broadsword through his skull.

Through the mist and darkness, Hervor could not see it as Kare's body fell.

And now the rage was on her, and terror had fled. Chest heaving with fury, she raced up the hill. Kare. Another of Haki's champions. A man she'd fought side by side with for long moons.

Cut down by this ... Walking Kraken.

Well, she would test his invincibility on Tyrfing.

With a battle cry, she charged in, swung as fast as she could. Her left-handed attacks might have been clumsy, a little off-balance. But then, she had but to scratch the bastard and he'd be dining with Hel.

The Walking Kraken spun on her, his movements swift and yet slightly stiff. Almost pained-seeming.

Hrethel came up the slope behind her, three of his men alongside him.

Hervor nodded at them. "We'll take this bastard together."

After offering a grim nod in return, Hrethel moved to

flank their foe, his men breaking off to either side. No one was taking chances after what they'd heard. What they'd seen him do to Kare.

The champion's body lay sunken into the snow as Hervor passed, wishing she could spare the time to say some words for him. Soon. Once the Walking Kraken was done walking.

The man lurched into sudden movement. Swung at Hervor. Drove her back.

He twisted his attack almost immediately. A feint—one that let him cleave into one of Hrethel's men. The broadsword slammed against the man's helm, scraped down, and tore into his chin. The poor bastard toppled over, screaming and clutching his split face.

Snarling, Hervor struck.

Her foe moved too fast, twisted out of the way of her clumsy attack, and spun around to engage another of Hrethel's men. This one he caught by the arm and yanked, sent the man tumbling down the hill. And then he was back around, fending off attacks from Hrethel and the remaining man.

Well, they'd give Hervor the chance to end him. She kept Tyrfing low to the ground as she edged forward. Circling. Waiting for the chance ...

Kraken's broadsword clanged down on Hrethel's shield. Same time, he jerked his elbow back into the other man's face. The thegn's nose exploded in blood, and he pitched over backward, tumbled end over end, and rolled down the hill.

Hervor raced in, made a tight swing at Kraken's legs.

He jumped over her attack, his knee colliding with her sternum. The force of it sent her stumbling backward. Gasping for air.

Felt like getting kicked by a horse, straight in the chest.

Odin's balls, this man was strong.

Hrethel did not waste the opportunity, though.

Roaring, the jarl embedded his own sword deep into the man's back. The Kraken jerked from the impact. Then he spun and caught Hrethel on the side of his helm with one hand. The impact rang out like a gong. Hrethel spun round twice and dropped like a stone to the hillside. Rolled through the snow, down the slope.

The Kraken grasped the blade in his back with one hand, fingers not even seeming to feel the blade as they closed around the edge. A single jerk tore it free, and he tossed it aside.

Hel. That was what Hervor was afraid of. If Jorund had draugar in his army, it only made sense his champion would be one, too.

One of the men Kraken had knocked down was struggling to rise. Never make it back up here in time.

It fell on her, then.

And she was going to fucking die.

Hervor spit, then charged. The draug batted her sword aside with his own, stepped inside, and caught her left shoulder with his free hand. All one swift motion.

He pulled her backward, then slammed the pommel of his broadsword into her chest.

All the wind exploded from her lungs. Brilliant white light clouded her vision, and her legs gave out beneath her.

Couldn't ... breathe ...

"I'm ... going ... to make you suffer ..." The raspy voice echoed in her ringing head. Hard to make sense of it.

Couldn't breathe ...

The draug dropped her.

It stepped back. Waiting. Until, gasping and choking, she finally managed to look up at it.

And it slowly pulled back the hood, revealing those fell, gleaming red eyes. That rotting face ...

The face she knew.

Orvar-Oddr. The Arrow's Point.

The Walking Kraken was ... invincible ... because he was Arrow's Point ... back from the dead.

Hervor tried to speak. To protest. To deny it. All she managed was a choking cough and spitting up blood. She pitched forward, heaving as more blood dribbled out of her mouth.

The foul creature knelt beside her. "I'm not going ... to kill you ... until all you love ... has crumbled ... to dust ... until you beg ... for death."

Hervor sucked down a painful breath. Patted around for Tyrfing. Where was it? Where was her sword!

"And then ... you shall join me ... in eternal torment."

Shouts, war cries rang out from beyond the hill. More men coming to aid her.

Too late.

Orvar's foot snapped up into her face.

White light exploded before her eyes. And then darkness.

28

Through the blood and chaos of the battle, Starkad pushed on. He'd lost track of how many of Jorund's men he'd slain. Draugar, those he counted. Three of them, and each more difficult than the last.

Only Ecgtheow by his side—wielding that runeblade—only he had managed to finally slay the deathless, vile abominations. Starkad could not begin to fathom how Jorund had harnessed such dark powers. Sorcery? The only ones Starkad knew of who could control draugar were the Niflungar.

Those sorcerers were the nightmares of his childhood, and ancient inviolable power, woken by Odin. Driven to mad rage. If not for the Niflungar, maybe Mother would have yet lived. Maybe Vikar ... maybe he and Starkad would not have left the Aesir ... maybe ...

Starkad shook his head to clear it.

Battle fatigue was driving him into delirium. Focus. Be fast—faster than the draugar. He had to find Jorund and end this.

With one blade, he swept an axe away. The other, he

slapped against his foe, the flat of the blade clanging against the man's helm. The stunned warrior fell to his knees, and Starkad kicked his weapon away.

"Where is your king?" Starkad demanded.

His only answer was a groan. He drove a sword down through the man's exposed neck. A hot spray of blood squirted over him.

"Ecgtheow!"

The man was at his side a moment later, drenched in blood. Chest heaving.

Starkad was almost glad for the darkness. Glad he could not see how close to giving in to exhaustion his ally must be. "I cannot find Jorund in this."

Ecgtheow leaned over, hands on his knees, and shook his head. "Only draugar ... benefit from fighting ... at night."

Well, them and varulfur and aught else spawned from the Otherworlds. Many such powers preferred the cover of night, if not outright weakened by the sun's rays. Starkad paused for a moment. Beings like ... svartalfar.

Was it possible?

A flicker of insight, a waking dream. A vision in his mind, pulling him forward through the valley. Forward. Bent toward an urd he could not deny, perhaps not so unlike the very power that made men call Odin a god.

Blades flashing, Starkad battled his way past more men, another draug. He drove this one down, hacked off its legs. Left it for Ecgtheow to finish.

There was darkness.

Deeper than the night, deeper than total blackness. For it was the living dark. The same power that had corrupted Starkad's life and damned him to his cursed existence. The same power ... that Volund had embraced, decades ago, in the deep forge of Njarar.

The power ... his son had called upon.

And there, at the heart of the next valley, surrounded by the swirling shadows, Wudga stood. Ecgtheow approached behind Starkad, bearing a torch that ought to have extended twice the light it did. It ought to have let Starkad see clearly the foes before him. But even the light feared what dwelt in this valley.

If Starkad turned back as his heart urged him, the darkness here would spread and spread. Like any other vaettir, svartalfar meant humanity ill and would search for a foothold into Midgard to wreak havoc upon it. Now, it seemed, Wudga had given them such an opportunity.

"What did you use the eitr for?" Starkad shouted at the man he had once trusted.

Wudga strode forward, the blade in his hand gleaming with faint light, runes radiant. Yes, his skin, his hair, all had become like his father's. Like a svartalf.

"What was it for?" Starkad repeated.

Wudga stalked closer, his face masked in shadows. "Power ... conquest ... what else?"

"You're serving them?"

"Them?" Wudga chuckled. "Yes, *them*. They are patient, Starkad. They have waited long for the chances I provide ... for the chance to find a suitable ruler to advance their own empire."

Starkad edged around him, keeping his blades up. "Their empire? Through Jorund?"

"Surely you realize the age of man is ending. Our world has been dying for millennia."

"The Old Kingdoms—"

"Were a disease. A feeble attempt to forestall the coming end of humanity by making pacts with the very powers set to overthrow mankind. They were blights that destroyed themselves, as all the realms of man must invariably do. For the human race to persist, there is but one chance ... to return to its natural state."

Starkad blanched. "You mean ... as hosts to vaettir? As slaves?"

"Is that not the very reason for your race's creation? Your very purpose of existence is but to sate the needs and whims of the greater powers beyond. And the walls keeping them back begin to crumble ..."

The words might have held some fragment of truth. But they turned Starkad's stomach. Some things could not be accepted. Some things must be fought against, even if a final victory proved impossible. Even urd might be resisted, for a time. "You were ... you *are* still human, Wudga. You do not have to take your father's path. You do not have to walk so far in the dark you forget the light."

"How do you know it is not too late already?"

"Because I want to believe the man I fought alongside ... the man I knew ... might still be in there."

Wudga chuckled again, the sound dark and vile. "Then come to me. And find out."

Damn it.

Left with no choice, Starkad charged forward. Twisted. One blade and then another. Wudga fell back under his sudden, relentless assault. The man faltered, clearly struggling to parry two swords with his single blade.

Again and again Starkad launched his blows, ever aiming to wear Wudga down. His foe grimaced, losing more ground, but did not fall. Twice, Starkad could have ended it; he knew he could have. Wudga's runeblade dropped a little too low, a little out of place.

But that would mean killing a man he'd liked, a man he'd called friend.

Not that Starkad had not done so before. But ... never again. Not if he could help it. Starkad was done murdering on Odin's behalf. He needed to be better ...

Wudga twisted around with frightening speed and shrieked as he brought Mimung down against Starkad's sword. The blade, the sword Tyr had given him, snapped in half under the runeblade's blow. Starkad gaped at the shards of it. For so many years, he'd carried this weapon ... his one token from his days among the Aesir.

Roaring, Wudga jerked Mimung back around, swinging at Starkad's head. The assault yanked Starkad from his momentary grief, and he leapt backward, tossing the useless hilt aside.

And now Wudga launched his own unending stream of attacks. Faster and stronger than Starkad would have judged him. One move flowed into the next with Otherworldly grace and inhuman fury. Shadows darted around Starkad's foe, obscuring his face, making his moves hard to read.

Now bearing only Vikar's sword, Starkad struggled to keep up. To parry, to dodge. Wudga swung overhead at Vikar's blade, seeming intent to destroy it as well. Starkad lurched out of the way, then toppled backward onto his arse.

"Submit willingly," Wudga said. "They would approve of a host with your skills."

Starkad blanched. Was that what these svartalfar wanted here? Hosts to possess? Was that what had happened to Jorund?

But not Wudga ... Wudga had always had it in his blood. He wasn't possessed. He was making a choice to become what his father before him had become. To welcome in the powers of the dark.

And Wudga seemed inclined to give Starkad a moment

to ponder his so-called offer. As if any sane man might even consider allowing a vaettr to possess his body.

Starkad scrambled to his feet and held Vikar's sword out before him. "I'm going to kill Jorund. And if I judge the situation well ... I'd be doing him a favor. Even passing through the gates of Hel might not be worse than the urd he has taken upon himself."

Wudga sneered, the expression made all the more unnerving by the writhing shadows coating his face like oil.

"You, though," Starkad said. "You, Wudga, might still avoid that end."

The man scoffed, though he'd failed to fill it with as much disdain as Starkad might have expected. More ... resignation.

"I am my father's son."

Starkad circled him. "I believed that. Once ... I thought myself Bedvig's son, and I hated Tyr for his death. Then I thought myself Tyr's son ... but he turned his back on me. And I realized ... we are who we choose to be."

"Oh. So you chose the life of murder and betrayal, the slaughter of those close to you? The endless wandering under the weight of your fell urd, Starkad? Oh yes, the shadows know you well, Eightarms. For few men have so much blood on their hands in all of Midgard."

Starkad wanted to deny that. Wanted to call himself a victim ... but even were it true, it would undermine the very argument he'd hoped to make with Wudga. Besides. Wudga spoke too much truth to ignore. "No, you're right ... I did bring my urd upon myself. I walked into darkness, as you have. And still, I struggle against it. As you could, if you but chose to."

"To what end? The prince has his sights set upon

Midgard now, and Sviarland offers the perfect staging ground."

Prince? A svartalf prince? "The prince is ... inside Jorund?" Starkad let Vikar's sword drop a hair.

Wudga snickered then, shaking his head. "You still don't understand, Starkad. I told you ... they have use for a strong host. One with the strength to take this world and hold it until the end of time."

Starkad's legs felt weak. His stomach lurched at the words. This svartalf prince ... wanted him. How did they know of him at all? Had Volund told him? Or ... no. He wouldn't have needed to. Starkad had spent years building his reputation as the most famed mercenary in the North Realms. And he already courted the darkness ... Odin had introduced him to it, long ago.

"Was it ... was it even chance you hired me to help you kill Otwin?"

"Of course not. Why do you think Father suggested I call upon you? They have known you all these years, watched you."

"Your father has embraced the darkness ... but he was born on this world. So I rather think it means he can die. As he will, should he come before me again. As for you, Wudga ..."

The man shook his head. "Part of me wishes you were right, Starkad. But ... no. There is no stopping Rathwith now. And when Mimung has tasted your blood and you lie dying ... I imagine you will accept most any bargain to preserve your wretched life. And you will serve the prince."

Now Starkad shook his head. He almost pitied Wudga. The fool had been caught in the web of beings more powerful and ancient than he could understand. Perhaps it was too late to save him. Perhaps the best Starkad could offer was death while some glimmer of humanity yet remained to Wudga.

He raised his blade again.

Scowling, Starkad's foe charged back in.

Starkad fell into the defensive. Dodging. Parrying. The occasional riposte.

He would truly have to kill Wudga ...

Another man he'd thought a friend. Another murder. Another step into the darkness.

Just. Like. Wudga.

Starkad let his guard drop a little. Wudga seized the chance, swinging at Vikar's sword, clearly intent to sunder it as he had Starkad's own heirloom. Starkad jerked his sword away at an angle, caught Mimung on the cross guard, and twisted. Round and round he spun the blades, winding and binding, until Wudga's face creased in consternation. The svartalf clearly had not expected the wild move. Too reckless. Just how Starkad liked it.

With a heave, Starkad jerked both swords away. Mimung flew from Wudga's hand and dunked into a snowdrift.

This was it.

He could end Wudga here, now.

And still the svartalf prince and Jorund would continue their conquest of Sviarland.

Starkad tossed his own sword aside. Wudga eyed him a moment. Starkad feinted one way, then swung at Wudga's jaw with an uppercut. The blow slammed hard into the man, sending him tumbling to the ground. Starkad dropped down on him, knees first.

Then he rained blow after blow upon Wudga's face and chest and head.

Until the man lay still.

29

Twenty-Two Years Ago

*V*ikar had been right, of course. As had Ogn.

All hope had left Starkad.

Moons he wandered, crossing the land on foot, caring naught which way he went, or even if he travelled in circles. He passed out of Nidavellir and into Sviarland.

Sometimes, he passed through a village, a town. Sometimes they let him claim supplies without argument.

Sometimes they resisted. It ended poorly for them.

He fought, and he murdered, taking what he needed to survive.

Ogn had been his redemption. But she had fallen for her captor during Starkad's long absence and ... and was this all born of the curse Odin's blessing had brought with it? The dark fate Vikar had promised?

But then, as Ogn had said, he felt compelled to keep walking. He could not long abide any place, nor find peace among any of the villages or kingdoms he passed through. Her words haunted his every step.

As did death.

His dreams too, she invaded, on the rare occasion when Vikar did not torment him. On those times, it became Ogn's turn. And her suicide played out over and over, in innumerable variations. All coming to the same end—that precious light flickering out of her beautiful blue eyes.

The two people he'd thought he loved best in the world, both dead because of him.

Sometimes, he mulled over the idea of taking his own life. He might cast himself from a cliff into the sea. Or cut out his own gut with Vikar's sword—that would be justice. And yet, if he did so ... if he ended his suffering after betraying his own brother to ensure his long life ... would that not be further betrayal? If he had any honor left, it compelled him now to live.

To continue the cursed existence he had wrought for himself and live out the curses his loved ones had placed upon his soul. That was his punishment. And he would not shirk it.

So he walked, until he wore holes in the soles of his boots. Then he stole more boots and kept walking.

In long stretches alone, he was left with no companion save his own beleaguered mind. And left to wonder ... Ogn had known much of the workings of the Otherworlds. Had spoken of her fears that svartalfar had touched Starkad. Could that be ... was it possible she knew it because the others, the liosalfar, had touched her as well?

Skalds called those beings radiant and glorious, as had Ogn been. Maybe that hint of the Otherworldly was the source of her ethereal beauty and of the power behind her curse. Or maybe his mind tricked him, struggling to make sense of the ravages left of his life.

After long wanderings, he came to Upsal.

The kings there, brothers, Alrik and Eirik, welcomed him into their hall. Word of his crimes had spread yes but word of his glorious battles as well. Alrik had beckoned Starkad to sit on his right hand, offering him mead and hearty stew and song.

And the shieldmaidens and the slave women, they looked at him, wanton and willing.

And Starkad stared into the drinking horn.

He made a mistake with Ogn. Thought with his heart and his cock and placed all his hopes in her. But she had betrayed him as surely as he had Vikar. Women were fickle, not to be trusted. And Starkad had no need of them.

Just the mead. Drunk enough, and he'd not dream. Surely even he deserved that slight respite, on occasion.

A man settled across the table from him, then offered him a fresh horn. This man, his long, sandy brown hair tied at his neck, had a slightly fell edge about him. A power, an urd Starkad could not understand but could feel.

Starkad snatched the horn from him. "Who are you?"

"I'm Wudga Volundson. And I've heard a great many tales of your fame, Eightarms."

Volundson? As in ... the dark smith? Starkad snorted. Why not? Darkness seeped into every corner of Midgard. "What do you want?"

Wudga shrugged. "A good tale to pass the winter evenings? Perhaps friendship, even."

That drew a chuckle. "Can't say aught has ended well for my friends thus far."

Again, that relaxed shrug. "Perhaps this time will be different."

King Alrik banged a hand on the table, drawing every eye. "I have an inclination to raid into Kvenland soon. And tales of your many victories for Agder have become nigh to legend, Eightarms. Would you consent to become a captain among our party?"

Starkad slurped his mead and exchanged another glance with this Wudga.

So this is what his life was to be now. Odin had promised him great wealth. And Ogn had promised it would never be enough.

All those raids on behalf of Vikar, and what did it now earn him? Naught at all.

But then, the only question on his lips ... "How much is my share?"

For she was right.

Starkad could not hold back, could not stop from venturing forth to claim treasures he *knew* he would not be able to keep.

Such was his urd.

After all, he could not stay here long. He could not stay *anywhere* long.

30

hose touched by the Otherworlds carried fell powers mankind could not explain nor understand. Starkad had heard such powers could be suppressed with orichalcum chains. Having no such bindings, he'd been forced to rely on iron manacles to hold Wudga.

Now, they had all retreated to the hall of Hervor's grandfather, Jarl Bjalmar, who'd seemed aught but pleased to see Starkad. Still, finding his own forces beleaguered by Jorund's war bands, the jarl had agreed to take them in. Those of them who'd remained.

With the draugar at his side, Jorund had slaughtered half of Hrethel's army and routed the rest of them.

Hrethel had found Hervor unconscious, Jorund's champion gone. And so Ecgtheow and Hrethel and Inkeri all sat against the wall, watching, while a half-competent healer stitched a wound on Hervor's head outside.

While Starkad paced in front of Wudga where he lay, chained to the wall and stripped to the waist.

In the end, they were going to lose. If naught changed, Jorund would claim the thrones of Dalar and Ostergotland before winter was out. The king had bypassed Njarar only because he saw it as no threat—word had come that Olof Sharpsighted had claimed the vacated throne and more power to him. Surrounded on all sides, Olof would have no choice but to surrender and submit to Jorund.

And then, come summer ... well, the possessed king would surely move on Skane or Jamtla, if not both at once. Between his own army, the draugar, and whatever fell power the svartalf possessing him granted, Jorund seemed invincible.

None of it should have been Starkad's problem, though. He could have gone on to Holmgard, headed for Glae-sisvellir and claimed the damned runeblade like he'd planned. Except, he'd promised Hervor. And now they sheltered with her grandfather in lands the man would lose ... along with his life, no doubt.

Unless Starkad found a way to break Jorund's power.

He sighed. So.

Yanking a water skin from his belt, he popped the cork. Then he upended the contents over Wudga's head. The man sputtered awake, spitting and snarling.

At once, Ecgtheow and the others were on their feet, weapons in hand.

"I still don't see why we don't just kill this fucker," Ecgtheow mumbled.

Starkad leaned down across from his chained friend. "You thought no one could defeat their own nature or reject the darkness. But I beat you ... and I spared you. That ought to tell you something. Perhaps you yet have a choice, Wudga. When I leave here, I must leave you to make it."

Anger and doubt warred over Wudga's face. A rush of emotions ... but no unnatural shadows. Not yet.

The door opened, and Hervor slipped inside, nodded at Starkad, and shook her head at Wudga.

Starkad turned back to the man.

"Tell me how to defeat Jorund, my friend."

Wudga sneered, though the expression looked hollow, lacking confidence.

Starkad leaned in and grabbed the man's forearm. "You do have a choice. You always did. Even Volund had a choice —and he made the wrong one. I would know, Wudga—I have made my fair share of poor choices. Fuck, all men do, I guess."

"Women, too," Hervor mumbled from behind him.

Wudga swallowed hard. "There's no redemption."

Starkad shrugged. "Maybe not. Maybe the best you can do is make better choices going forward. Learn to live with the blood you've shed. I don't know, Wudga. But see ... if there is redemption, this would be a small measure of yours. I know you must have tricked Jorund into letting a svartalf possess him. But how has he achieved such victories so quickly? Is it the draugar? Did the svartalf prince grant those?"

"They came from Thule."

Thule? Damn it. So the horrors Starkad and the others had woken had found a way off the island. This, then, fell upon them.

Wudga shifted, groaning and working his swollen jaw. "Jorund is a pawn. Prince Rathwith controls him, and the draugar as well, though those came here following their own king."

Hervor groaned. Starkad could hardly blame her. Still, it should not surprise him that another draug had taken up the crown of the draug prince she and Orvar had slain.

Starkad frowned. "But Jorund is the face of this army. If I kill him ..."

"You cannot."

"Why?"

"Because I used the eitr you acquired to bathe his flesh in a brew that makes it impervious to harm."

Now Starkad groaned. "How did you even know how to ..." Well, that answer seemed obvious enough. Rathwith, a svartalf prince, must be privy to all manner of forgotten lore. "If such a technique exists, why not treat all of the army with it?"

"Because calling on the Art is draining, even for vaettir. Rathwith must maintain the power of it, and even that requires him to sustain himself on a constant banquet of souls. Fortunately, Jorund has fed him well, and the king and the prince both grow stronger with each life Jorund claims."

Now Hervor stalked closer and knelt beside them. "Surely not even this eitr can protect against Tyrfing."

Wudga glowered, shook his head. "No blade can harm him. Not even your precious runeblades, forged by the dvergar who, ancient in your eyes, are maggots before the likes of the svartalfar."

Hervor snatched up Wudga's chains and yanked him toward her face. "So you mean to say Jorund is unstoppable? I refuse to believe that."

"Believe what you will."

No. It would not end like this. Starkad eased Hervor's hands off of Wudga. "Rathwith is maintaining Jorund's invincibility, yes? So the prince must be in possession of a host here, on Midgard."

"Yes."

"One not so protected by the eitr."

"Oh, but he is awash in it. Flush with the power of creation and the fuel of hundreds of devoured souls."

Starkad leaned back. "Awash in eitr ... you mean ... in the same pool that you sent me to."

"You slew the guardian of the eitr."

Oh godsdamn it all. Wudga had tricked him from the beginning ... tricked him into slaying the dragon and opening the way for Rathwith to reach the eitr well. "So Rathwith bathes in the eitr and channels power to the svartalf possessing Jorund. But if Rathwith's host were slain ..."

Now Wudga chuckled without the least apparent humor. "You may bear two runeblades, but you cannot overcome Prince Rathwith or his guardians, my friend. Submit to him. He will shed his rotten host and take your body and through you, rule all of Sviarland. You'll be free to do with Jorund as it pleases you."

"Two runeblades ..." Starkad glanced at the others. "Tyrfing and Naegling ... and Mimung."

Wudga groaned. "So you'd take the very prize you fought to win me?"

"No. No, *you're* going to wield it. If you want to escape the urd that lies before you ... confront it. Fight it and slay it with that very sword. Wudga, take my word for it ... better to die fighting your terrors than live forever haunted by them in unending sleepless nights."

Ecgtheow cleared his throat. "Starkad. You and I and Hervor have faced our share of horrors, but this Rathwith sounds a good deal worse than even a draug prince."

"You cannot even begin to imagine," Wudga said. "Mortal man cannot hope to overcome a being of such ancient an inexorable malice. Rathwith has watched the passing of eons and more changings of the world than you can conceive of. We go to our deaths and, perhaps, worse.

He will feast on our very souls. Oblivion will be our fate—if we are lucky."

Ecgtheow coughed. "Right. Sounds encouraging. Are we certain no other option lies before us?"

Starkad stood. "I see none, though I surely cannot force any of you to come down this road."

"You're forgetting something," Hrethel said. "While we fight this Rathwith, Jorund only strengthens his hold on Sviarland. You may go off hunting, but someone has to remain to delay his advance."

"In a fight you cannot possibly win?" Ecgtheow said. "I would not see my father-in-law meet Odin quite so soon."

Starkad barely managed to bite his tongue. Somehow, he doubted Odin arranged Valhalla for anyone. If Valhalla even existed. If aught besides the gates of Hel possibly awaited those fallen in battle.

Hrethel shook his head. "Jorund and Eikkr spent a great deal of time pillaging along the coasts of Nidavellir before their father's death. They made more than one enemy back then, even killed King Gudlög. Perhaps I can enlist some who would welcome any chance for vengeance."

From what Starkad remembered, Gudlög had been more pirate than king, but he supposed any ally was a boon at this point. He rose. "Hervor, go with him. Help him find Gudlög's people."

She scoffed. "I'll do no such thing. You need Tyrfing, and the sword does not leave my sight."

"You can barely fight."

"I am recovering—"

"You'll die!" And that Starkad could not allow. Not again. Not again.

"If you plan to take Wudga with you, you need someone

to keep an eye on him." The pair of them had locked gazes. "Someone to run him through if he betrays you again."

Starkad waited, hoping Wudga would protest that he'd not do any such thing. But Volund's son said naught, just stared daggers at Hervor. Finally, Starkad shook his head. "No man would question your bravery, Hervor. But you cannot—"

"No, Starkad. You cannot tell me where I can and cannot go. Jorund has slain my king, and he … well, I have sworn to see him dead. And if I must go through Prince Rathwith, then so be it. I am coming with you."

Stubborn fool of a woman.

One he could not stand to lose.

31

*H*ervor's torch sputtered as they wandered back down these dark tunnels. She had not thought to return here, nor did the descent hold less fear the second time. No, this time, they knew what to find in the old dverg ruin, and it would be worse even than the dragon they'd slain before. This time, the dark prince awaited them.

All too soon, they returned to the black pit and the spiral path descending into the darkness. Ecgtheow came up beside her, peering down into the abyss, while Wudga shied away from the pair of them ... or from their torches. Inkeri hung yet farther back, clutching her own torch like it might preserve her from this nightmare. Ought to have left her behind. The shieldmaiden was brave enough, without doubt, but few—men or women—could handle places like this without breaking.

Hervor wasn't sure she herself could.

And Starkad ... well, naught seemed to frighten him. Already, he had begun his descent along that path. Forcing Hervor to follow. She had insisted on coming along, after all.

"Going down there, I take it," Ecgtheow said.

Hervor did not bother answering the pointless question, instead slowly making her way after Starkad.

Somehow, the torches seemed even less effective at driving back the darkness this day than they had on her first visit to this cursed ruin. Somehow ... and she knew how, much as every instinct in her gut wanted to deny it was even possible. Oh, she had seen awful things on Thule and now here in Sviarland, and still ... the human mind did not want to believe it might share the world with such abominations.

At the path's end, Starkad had drawn up short, staring out into the chamber they'd descended around.

Another man lay enwrapped in the coils of the dead dragon, half submersed in the pool, flesh the color of old ash, and hair black as pitch. His squinting eyes reflected the torchlight, gleaming an unearthly yellow. Black fluid dribbled out of his mouth and over his chin.

So transfixed was she at the sight, only when another person groaned did she see it—naked men and women, chained along the boundary of the pool. Numerous cuts marred their flesh, and blood dribbled slowly to mix in with the water. Hervor stifled a gasp as more of the horror came into focus. Strange runes painted in blood spread out in a ring around the prisoners, a perverse circle she could not have imagined in her worst nightmares. To even gaze upon those symbols set her mind squirming in protest, and they seemed to move as she looked at them.

And now, amidst shifting shadows, other forms moved. Two, maybe three of these svartalfar.

"Eikkr?" Ecgtheow said. Hervor had not even realized he'd drawn up behind her.

As he did, as they all did, the torches dimmed further, lengthening the shadows until Hervor could almost pretend the profane ritual did not exist. And yet some visions could not be unseen.

The being enmeshed with the dragon corpse chuckled, the sound reverberating through the chambers, as if the darkness itself cast its echoes. "The body is ... a vessel."

Starkad took a step off the path, now armed with a sword granted by Hrethel as well as one of the ones he'd carried before. "I'm going to kill you now."

Again, that fell chuckle that might have unnerved Hel herself. "Boy, I have watched you since the paltry and self-important king of the Aesir called upon us on your behalf. I have watched you slaughter and bleed this world dry and waited ... and here, I thought I would send my servants to claim you. But instead, you deliver yourself to me freely. And soon, I shall shed this rotting carcass and claim that which I invested in back then."

"My son," another of the shadows said. From that direction, limped out another svartalf. Despite his obviously lame leg, he moved with a grace and vitality that shamed Rathwith's sickly looking form. "You seem to have grown confused, but at least you brought your subject back here at last."

Wudga strode forward, Mimung in hand, a not-quite-concealed tremble shaking the blade as he drew up beside Starkad.

Hervor reached for Tyrfing. If Wudga betrayed them now ...

"I made another choice, Father."

"Urd is not about choices, my son ... I fear you must learn that one day or another."

"Enough banter," Rathwith said. "Submit to me now, Starkad, and I will grant your companions a swift death and even allow their souls to pass from this realm without molestation. You cannot hope for a more generous offer. For I have spent eons steeping in the lightless realms, absorbing the mysteries of the dark, until I have become one with shadow. Deny me, and through those shadows, I shall rip the secrets from your minds and the light from your bodies, leaving naught but hollowness fit to serve the dark."

Starkad took another step forward. "I cannot escape the dark. Perhaps I never could ... but though damned, I still shall not bend to your will, wretch."

Rathwith cackled wheezily. He was feeding so much of his energy to Jorund that maybe ... if they struck fast ...

The svartalf prince clenched his fists.

Every torch they carried winked out.

Leaving them in total darkness.

32

*O*h fuck.

Starkad faltered, unable to make out aught in the chamber. Just sounds. The soft pad of boots on stone, the shifting of leather and mail. The moaning of the victims from Rathwith's ritual.

And then pale light flared up into the cavern. In Hervor's hand, Tyrfing cast its fell gleam through the chamber.

A svartalf not a foot from Starkad hissed at the sudden flare of light.

Wasting no time, Starkad spun, a swipe of his sword taking the vaettr's head from his shoulders.

Volund shambled away from him, and Wudga stepped up, driving his father further into the darkness. The man had hardly earned Starkad's trust ... but under such circumstances, Starkad had little choice.

Hervor drew up beside Starkad while Ecgtheow and Inkeri began to flank Rathwith, clearly not the least bit intent to close in on that poison pool.

Starkad, however, had survived those toxins before. And he'd do it again if needs be. "I don't think you can leave the pool, can you? Does the eitr sustain that corpse you've possessed? Or would stepping away merely break Jorund's invincibility? In either case ... the Yngling king will not endure long once I send your screaming soul back into the darkness of the Otherworld."

Rathwith sneered. "You were not listening at all, boy. I told you ... I dwelt long in darkness, until all its secrets unfolded before me." The svartalf prince heaved like a man about to retch. And then, indeed, his whole body seemed to vomit at once, expelling from it a shadow. An umbral duplicate of the svartalf, armed with a sword of darkness. Only a hint of Rathwith's features persisted in this entity. The shadow copy walked upon the pool's surface and strode out to meet Starkad.

"I'll deal with this *thing*," Starkad said. "Hervor, kill the prince."

"Gladly."

But the shadow before Starkad writhed and then ruptured, split into a copy of itself that broke away and moved in on Hervor. While Rathwith vomited out another of the shadowy likenesses of himself.

Well. Fuck.

Bellowing a war cry, Starkad charged at the nearest of the creatures. It jerked its blade up, and Starkad's own clanged upon it, ringing out like he'd struck actual iron. Indeed, this creature moved almost like a being of flesh and blood, despite its features seeming fluid and concealed. Roaring, Starkad launched attack after attack, driving the shadow creature backward.

And still, it was fast, skilled with that blade, as if possessed of Rathwith's immeasurable years of practice. Other shadow effigies had engaged Hervor, Ecgtheow, and

Inkeri, while Wudga had disappeared into the darkness in pursuit of Volund.

And how many more of these creatures could Rathwith create? An army?

No.

If he could do that, he'd not have needed a mortal army. Indeed, the svartalf convulsed and grew even more ashen as Starkad's allies fought against the shadows. So even this ancient creature had its limits. And Starkad was going to find them.

He rained blows upon the shadow until, at last, he managed to knock down the sword with one of his own. Vikar's sword lanced up and opened the creature's throat. It fell back a few steps. Shuddered. And then came at Starkad again.

No blood.

It moved like flesh ... but it was not flesh.

Now Starkad dropped backward. No flesh ... it could not die? It was hardly Starkad's wont to pray ... but now ...

Not that Odin could even hear prayers.

Roaring, Starkad advanced back in. The shadow had grown yet faster, more aggressive. That fell blade darted out again and again, until it gashed Starkad's arm. An icy chill shot up his limb and filled his neck, seeming to choke him. Every breath became pained.

"Fucking die!" Starkad continued to fall back, letting the creature press its attack.

Then he twisted out of the way and swung down with his good arm. His newly granted blade sheared through the shadow's arm at the elbow. The shadow's sword vanished into nothingness its severed arm going with it. With its other arm, it lurched for Starkad's throat. Starkad lopped that one off too.

Even as it came on, its first arm grew back out of the darkness, followed by a new blade. A replacement for its second arm.

"They call *you* Eightarms ..." The sound hissed from the shadow, but it was Rathwith's voice.

And now, another pair of arms jutted from his foe and another sword to match. And again and again, until the shadow creature truly had eight arms and four blades.

Starkad spared the barest glance at the real Rathwith, unreachable beyond the monstrosity that now barred Starkad's way. The svartalf prince convulsed. Black cracks now split his flesh, weeping some foul oil—perhaps more of the eitr itself. But the shadow before Starkad had risen up, well over seven feet tall. Blades of darkness cleft the air, forcing him into an endless series of dodges, parries. Lacking the slightest chance to counter.

If only he could ... creating these things was weakening Rathwith. So if Starkad could cut it down enough times ...

But then, he'd likely get himself lopped in half before Rathwith gave out. Nor could Starkad keep his own speed up forever. Not like this.

Across from him, Inkeri shrieked. The effigy she fought had hacked its blade across her guts. Now, it stooped, snatched her up, and carried her to the pool of eitr.

"No!" Starkad pushed forward, tried to get to her. His efforts only earned him a gash along his face. Seeping cold and darkness leeched his strength.

The effigy dropped Inkeri into the pool. Rathwith shuddered with obvious pleasure, a hint of vigor coming back into his failing form.

The monstrous shadow engaging Starkad swung even faster now, and Starkad scrambled away. His foot slipped in some muck, and he caught himself on the wall. Nowhere left to go.

Hervor bellowed and drove Tyrfing point first through the chest of the shadow facing her. The creature shuddered. It rent apart and dissolved like smoke. And the abomination closing in on Starkad faltered. Slowed ever so slightly.

Starkad rolled away, getting space between himself and that thing.

Rathwith had focused most of his energy upon Starkad, knew him for the best fighter. And had not taken into account the runeblades Hervor and Ecgtheow wielded.

The shadow that had slain Inkeri now closed in on Hervor.

"Give me Tyrfing!" Starkad shouted at her.

"I will not!" The shieldmaiden raced forward, engaging the next shadow.

Damn it. "I can end this!"

Hervor offered no answer, and the next instant, the eight-armed shadow was back on Starkad, forcing him onto the defensive once again.

Even with Tyrfing, Hervor's wounds kept her from fighting as she once had. This wasn't going to work. Not like this.

Starkad dared to steal a glance at Ecgtheow, but the shadow he faced had begun to fight more defensively, clearly wary of the runeblade.

As the monstrosity closed in again, Starkad rolled past it. If he could make it to Rathwith ... the shadow's blades flashed, and Starkad had to throw himself to the floor. He landed in blood or muck and slid along until he collided with one of the chained victims, tangled himself in her limbs. She wailed, beating at him—driven mad by her suffering.

"Get off of me!" he bellowed.

The shadow giant stalked closer. It loomed over his head. Starkad lurched away, but one of the swords lanced down like a bolt of lightning. It drove through his shoulder and pinned him to the floor. The darkness clouded his eyes. The shadow blade ripped through him, crushing his body and soul with icy tendrils of agony. It suffused his flesh. It feasted on his mind.

Rathwith was in there.

In Starkad's skull, beating on his brain. Beating it down in submission.

Your form will be mine.

Starkad opened his mouth to protest. His tongue failed him. Ashes seemed to coat his throat. Twisting and crunching, like dead flesh choking him. And yet, squirming inside him. Seeking a way to claim him. His heart seized up, threatened to give out.

Not like this.

Your body ... your skills ... they will unleash a new era of the dark. The shadows spread ...

Couldn't breathe. Blackness clouded his eyes.

Hervor. Hervor could help him if she ... if she ...

The shadow monster twisted that blade in his shoulder, sending waves of torment crashing over him.

She cannot help you ... I will feast upon her soul for days on end, until naught remains but a shriveled husk ...

He tried to scream. Managed a faint moan. Turned his head, ever so slightly.

Hervor fell beneath her shadow's onslaught, slipped to the floor. The shadow twisted its blade in a masterful move, and Tyrfing clattered from her hand. Its light dimmed, slowly winking out. To leave them all in darkness.

Starkad had failed.

The shadow monster impaling him shuddered. Then it melted into a sudden pool of oily darkness and was gone.

Starkad sucked down an agonizing breath.

In Tyrfing's last, fading light, he managed to roll over.

Wudga stood above Rathwith, having driven Mimung through the back of the prince's neck. A twist of Wudga's runeblade popped the svartalf's head from his shoulders.

And darkness settled in.

33

otal blackness had fallen upon the chamber. It left Hervor with naught to focus on save the moans of the wounded, the dying. The putrid stench of shit and urine and blood and other foulness she could not even identify, mixing with the rot of a decaying dragon.

Gasping, she dragged herself through the filth, daring to hope that ... what? That'd she'd find a torch cast aside somewhere in the massive cavern. That, despite it like as not being coated with filth and her unable to see, she'd light it.

Her fingers brushed over cold metal. Engraved.

Tyrfing's pommel.

Odin be praised! Hervor yanked herself over to the blade and grabbed it. Pale light began to radiate first from the runes, then the blade, seeming impossibly bright after the absolute darkness she'd just endured.

She rolled over.

Ecgtheow was nearby, clutching a wound on his neck. Other, less threatening gashes marred his face and arms. He'd have a great many scars from this day ... assuming losing all that blood did not yet kill him.

Indeed, Hervor brushed a hand over her own face. Scratches marred her cheek and another along her brow.

Starkad lay on his back, hand pressed over a wound in his shoulder. How he was even still awake after that ... if she didn't know better, she'd have thought he had the constitution of an Ás.

And there was Wudga, cleaning Mimung. Volund had forged that new runeblade, the first new one in ages. And now, Volund's own son had used it to kill the svartalf prince. And maybe Volund himself? Could Wudga have slain his own father?

Groaning, she sat up.

"Where's Volund?" Starkad asked before Hervor had the chance.

Wudga stared at him a moment. His eyes darted to Mimung. What the fuck was he thinking now? Might he yet betray them? A moment ago, she'd have thought his loyalty assured, having turned on Rathwith, having slain him. But now ... ?

Finally, Wudga shook his head. "Vanished into the darkness. Such is his way."

And just how hard had Wudga truly pursued his father? Well, if he'd let the man escape, Hervor could not entirely blame him for it. No one wanted to slay his or her own kin. It was an abomination before the eyes of gods and men. Unnatural.

"Starkad?" she asked. "Can you walk?"

He kept sucking down these long, slow breaths, like each was agony. They no doubt were. After Geigad had wounded her in the Fyris Wood, part of Hervor had wished for death with every passing hour. Would Starkad now suffer the same? A pair of cripples who ought to have died in battle?

"Give me a moment," Starkad finally said.

"I wonder if valkyries saw all that," Ecgtheow mumbled.

Wudga trudged over to where Starkad lay and offered him a hand. The other man finally took it, and Wudga pulled him up, even as Hervor struggled to gain her own feet.

"He was ..." Starkad shuddered in such obvious pain that Hervor wanted to go to him. To ease it in some way, though naught she could offer would do so. "I felt him ... deep in my head. I could feel him, crushing me from the inside. Had you taken but a moment more, maybe he'd have had me. Had you not killed him ..."

"Killed him?" Wudga snorted. "One does not kill a vaettr, Starkad. You ought to know this. I merely destroyed his host and forced his essence back into Svartalfheim. But Rathwith will endure ... and I doubt he will soon forgive any of us for this slight. Nor forget his designs upon you. If he already felt you giving in ... he is like to come for you again. I do not envy you that."

Hervor shuddered at Wudga's words.

THE WALK to the surface seemed longer, especially with all of them so wounded. It gave Hervor far too much time to dwell on what Wudga had said. If you could not kill a vaettr, if they were truly immortal, then how could you ever hope to win?

The answer she kept coming back to was so vexing that, at one point, she'd had to stop and vomit out what little she had in her stomach.

However, vexing, the answer was simple.

Mankind could not defeat vaettir.

They had eternity to work with. And thus undying,

sooner or later, they would win. It seemed inevitable—and most were barely aware of the Otherworlds.

Hervor did not expect her dreams to be more pleasant in the nights to come.

ْ◆

THEY SPENT a fortnight recovering in a nearby town.

Starkad should have died from his wounds, but he grew stronger and stronger. It made it hard to deny the truth of Rathwith's words, that something of the Otherworlds had touched Starkad. Made him fell in addition to granting him longer life. And Hervor could not decide whether to envy or pity him for that.

She still didn't have the answer when Hrethel arrived there, accompanied by a small force.

"Whatever you did," the jarl said, "it seems to have worked."

Starkad said naught, didn't rise from where he sat beneath an elm, glowering, as he did most often these days.

Hervor, however, nodded. "So Jorund can be defeated?"

"I don't know. But he seems less bold, and rumor circulates he sustained a wound in the assault on Dalar."

Ecgtheow clapped Hrethel on the shoulder. "If he can be wounded, he can die."

Once, Hervor had believed that. Rathwith had her doubt it now.

Hrethel cleared his throat, nodded at Ecgtheow. "Still. He has a large army, and the other kingdoms have suffered many losses of late. And at least a few of these draugar yet serve him." Hrethel turned to a man beside him. "This is Gylaug, son of Gudlög. He brought several ships with him from Nidavellir. They await us, ready to take us to Upsal."

Gylaug nodded, eyes filled with hatred Hervor knew all too well. Jorund had murdered his father, and he planned vengeance. She could hardly blame him.

But if Orvar-Oddr still worked alongside Jorund … "What of those draugar?"

Now, Starkad did rise, at last stalking to her side. "I will deal with Jorund myself. You and Ecgtheow bear the runeblades, and you must break the draugar or at least hold them back."

Gylaug sneered. "I must be there to see my father avenged. I must strike his slayer with my own hand."

"You and I then," Starkad said. "Wudga?"

Volund's son had shown himself rarely in their days resting, but he now stepped out from behind the tree, looking grim as ever.

"Will you fight with us?" Starkad asked.

Wudga shrugged, then ran fingers along Mimung's hilt. "I will see this done. And then I think I shall seek my fortune far from the shores of Sviarland. I have spent too long here already."

"So be it," Starkad said. "Are we all agreed?"

Hrethel nodded. "We must slay Jorund before he burns down all of Sviarland."

"We owe the bastard," Ecgtheow said. "He deceived and betrayed us … I have to right that."

And Hervor's oath demanded she finish the Yngling dynasty, even had Jorund not murdered Haki. And he had. Starkad was looking at her though. Waiting for an answer. "You know where I stand."

Starkad nodded. "Then we make for the sea. And we end this."

34

The draug's fist slammed into Hervor's mail and sent her toppling over backward, breath blasting out of her chest. Whole damned room spun.

Her head collided with the floor inside the Upsal hall. Here, in the very center of the power of her foes, on the eve of victory, she was going to die.

Groaning, she tried to rise.

Every fucking muscle in her body felt like it had been pummeled by a snow bear.

The draug fixed her with its Otherworldly gaze. And did not advance.

Hervor shook herself, sucking down painful breaths. Why wasn't it ...

It had paused halfway across the room ... refusing to pass through a beam of sunlight that streamed in from a window. Starkad had been right about them remaining indoors during the daylight. Even on Thule, the draugar had vanished for the few hours the sun had risen.

Why? Did it harm them?

With another grunt of effort, she regained her feet, Tyrfing in hand. "Afraid?"

The draug hissed at her. Maybe it understood Northern, maybe not. Didn't really matter.

Throughout the hall, the sounds of battle rang out. Outside, iron clashed on iron, and men shouted, died. Starkad had insisted they attack at dawn, said it would give them the advantage. While Hrethel fought the mortal army and Starkad hunted Jorund, Hervor and Ecgtheow had to scour the hall for draugar. Of course, neither Starkad nor Ecgtheow had any idea just *which* draug she feared the most.

The one she'd made herself.

A flourish of Tyrfing taunted the draug. Still, it did not cross the beam of light. Snarling at her. Growling and hissing some foulness one might expect beyond the gates of Hel.

The sunlight protected her ... but the draug barred the way into the rest of the hall. And Starkad had trusted Hervor to deal with this threat so he could focus on Jorund. Besides ... she had to find and kill Orvar before Starkad could see his old friend. Before that undead bastard could tell Starkad what she'd done.

Grimacing, she stalked forward to the edge of the light. She dipped Tyrfing into the sunbeam, twisted, until the light reflected on the draug's face. The creature hissed and fell back several steps. Hervor took the opportunity to lunge forward, shrieking and swinging for all she was worth. Tyrfing bit into the draug's gut and sent it shuddering backward.

She whipped the blade back around, severed its weapon arm. Then she roared and impaled the recoiling monster.

Tyrfing bit through its mail and rotten flesh with ease. The draug bellowed, caught her with its remaining hand, and hefted her body off the ground. It opened its putrid maw, exposing yellow teeth. The canines almost like fangs, dripping with steaming foulness. The draug pulled her closer and closer to his jaws.

Odin's balls! It was going to bite her face off. Hervor squirmed, unable to break its grip. She jerked on Tyrfing, and the blade tore free, taking a chunk of armor and skin and bone with it.

The draug buckled, letting her sink back to the ground. Roaring, she swung again, this time burying the blade into the draug's skull.

The sword wedged into bone, crunched it. As she tore it away this time, black goo oozed out from the draug's split head. And it dropped.

By Thor's cock, she hated these fucks. Panting, she collapsed against the wall. Too much to hope she'd have left all this behind on Thule. And now, no one but herself to blame. Orvar had brought these abominations to her homeland because of *her*.

So all she could do was find him and kill him again.

Sucking down another breath, she pushed off the wall and stalked back into the main feast hall. Dozens of men were engaged here, and at least three draugar, each slaughtering its way through the rapidly falling ranks of Hrethel's men. And there, Ecgtheow, driving back one of the draugar.

Hervor ought to join him. Together they could fight these off ... but then they'd find Orvar together too.

No. Damn it, she had to kill that bastard, and she'd have to leave Ecgtheow on his own to do it.

She pushed on, toward the back of the hall. Jorund and

Starkad were like to be back there, but maybe Orvar too, in service or partnership with the svartalf-possessed king. In truth, she cared little what their relationship or arrangement was. She needed them both dead, and she needed it done before the sun set this day.

This hall was larger than Haki's had been, with several side halls leading to private rooms no doubt assigned to members of the king's family, his housecarls, his guests. So she'd have to search every single one until she found—

A hand shot out of the shadows and snared her ankle in an iron grip. It tugged, sending her slamming face first into the ground. And then it heaved. Hervor spun through the air, everything blurring. She crashed through the wall and tumbled end over end into the adjacent chamber.

White light filled her vision.

Lungs not working.

Everything spinning.

She landed on her good shoulder. Had she broken her left arm now?

Spots danced before her eyes as she rolled over.

A man stalked the shadows, stepped out. Faint gleam in his eyes. The draug chuckled, the sound like knives slowly carving up her brain. Hervor managed to get a breath ... and promptly coughed up a wad of blood and phlegm. She'd ... bitten her tongue.

Orvar.

He stood over her, vile fangs bared. Tyrfing, clutched in one hand, dragging behind him.

"Ugh," she groaned. No. Not like this.

Hervor dragged herself away from the advancing draug. As if there was somewhere to go. As if a solid wall did not trap her in this building.

"Vengeance ..." The word bubbled out of Orvar's mouth, bloated and hissing.

Hervor whimpered, pulled herself up, lances of agony shooting through both arms at her effort. Her breath came in ragged gasps. Panic clutched at her chest. She had to get calm ... but staring into the face of such hatred stole all wit from her.

"It is all ... the damned can see. Not so unlike you ... perhaps you are one of us ... and did not yet know it ..."

Vengeance. It had brought her here. And damn her for her oath. But she'd sworn it, and she would not break it. Would not. Could not. Not even if it killed her.

Teeth grit against the agony of it, Hervor managed her feet. Spit out more blood. "I will ... fucking ... kill you ... again."

Orvar chuckled. And then he tossed Tyrfing at her feet. The golden-hilted blade skidded along the ground a moment before coming to rest a hair away from her. The draug fixed her with its fiery gaze as he pulled his own blade from over his shoulder. "Come to me then ..."

Still choking on the pain, Hervor knelt and snatched up Tyrfing. Its power flowed into her and almost, she imagined the suffering of her body diminished, dimmed the pain from all-consuming to mere mind-numbing. Blowing out a breath through clenched teeth, she raised Tyrfing before her foe.

Orvar edged closer.

Once, she had almost considered sparing the man. After hearing his tale, she might have ... were it not for her oath. Now though, no trace of humanity lingered in this rotten husk. It was an abomination born of the mist and consumed with hatred of life ... of her, most of all.

And she had to kill him now. Everything depended on it.

Hervor lunged forward, hewing with Tyrfing at Orvar's throat.

The draug batted her blade aside like she was a child. He caught her right arm, then spun her around and slammed her against the wall. Orvar yanked on her arm, pulled it up behind her back until it felt like it would snap off. The old wound in her neck and shoulder exploded in fresh agony, and Hervor whimpered.

Orvar crushed her face against the wall. Pushed her chest into it so hard she struggled to breathe. Sputtered, trying to form words.

He just bent her arm farther, and she screamed.

She heard his blade clatter to the ground. What was he ... did he intend to ...? Could a draug even ...?

She did not have long to dwell on his intent. Orvar grabbed the little finger of her right hand and bent it backward slowly.

Hervor's screams intensified.

The bone snapped with a sickening crunch, and flames of agony surged through her.

And the torture did not stop. The draug leaned in closer ... bent low, along the small of her back. Cold, sharp teeth brushed over her broken finger.

"Wha ...?" she whimpered.

The jagged teeth snapped down. They ripped through her flesh and crunched the bone.

She wailed in horror and blinding pain as her digit snapped off.

Orvar released her, and she slumped to her knees, clutching her hand and moaning.

"You ..." Blood dribbled down his chin as he crunched her finger with his teeth. "You ... have made me ... to suffer unending torment ... and eternal damnation. I can ... but return the favor."

She sucked another painful breath down and turned to glare up at him. "F-fuck ... you."

"Oh ... is that what you ... want from me?"

Her fingers closed around Tyrfing's hilt again. She didn't bother trying to still the tears as she rose. Suffering beyond all limits had stolen any chance of composure.

The draug just cackled again. "Yes ... come again ... and again ... and each time I shall steal ... a piece more ..."

Hervor bellowed. And she thrust Tyrfing through the wooden wall. The blade easily tore through the planks. Hervor jerked it downward, then slammed her arm into it, splintering it. Casting rays of sunlight into the room.

Orvar hissed, backed away.

Hervor threw herself at the wall. Crashed through it and fell into snows outside the hall.

Her breath fled once again, for an instant. A mere moment to catch it, and she was pulling herself along the ground, dragging her broken body through the snows.

And then a chill hand closed on her ankle once again.

What?

She turned back. Orvar stepped through the breach, batting away wood with his free hand.

"Y-you can't ..." she mumbled.

"Can't? Oh ... the sunlight steals the unearthly strength ... yes ... but to deal with you, Hervor. The strength ... of a man ... is more than enough."

No.

No.

No!

She beat helplessly at his grip around her ankle.

Orvar jerked her around and began to drag her away

from the Yngling hall. Snow slushed under her back. She flailed, unable to slow him in the least.

He pulled her through the burning gates in the wall. Warriors on both sides fought nearby, but none paid them much mind that Hervor could tell. All struggling to save their own lives.

The draug drew her into the Fyris Woods, and soon the snows gave way to icy bog waters. Hervor kicked at his wrist, but Orvar felt no pain. Or perhaps felt naught *but* pain now, and a few blows made no difference.

At last he dropped her, and she sunk in the marsh, the filth halfway up to her chin.

"I told you ... I will not kill you until you ... beg for it ... until all you love ... has fallen ..."

Orvar lurched forward. His clammy hand wrapped around her chin. He pushed and dunked Hervor's head into the bog.

Her battered lungs protested. They burned. And just when they would have exploded ...

He yanked her above the water again.

Gasping and panting, filth streaming into her mouth. Vile, dead waters and leeches and Odin knew what—

He shoved her back under again.

Hervor beat ineffectively at Orvar's arm.

Again and again.

Again the muck.

Her struggles became weaker. Only the next breath mattered. Only air ...

Orvar jerked her up out of the muck. "Cursed daylight ... saps the strength, you know ..." He slammed his fist into her gut.

Hervor heaved, retching up all she'd eaten and a good

deal of marsh water. The draug let her fall, and she splashed down again. And lay there.

Unable to move.

After a moment, Orvar leaned in close, his putrid clammy flesh pressing hers down into the muck. "I just want you to know ... this is only the beginning. My vengeance ... will last long ..."

And then he rose and slipped out between the trees.

Hervor shut her eyes and moaned.

35

Interrogating one of Jorund's men at swordpoint had led Starkad to a mine, abandoned long ago, but reopened now by the new king. And why not ... a man possessed by a svartalf would need a place to while away the daylight hours.

Gylaug walked beside him, holding his torch high, though its light hardly managed to fill this ancient tunnel. Spider webs clogged many of the passages, making their route obvious enough. Deeper into the darkness where their foe hid. Or waited, perhaps.

Blades in hand, Starkad pressed on. Time mattered much here, and he needed this to be done before sunset. Still, Jorund might lay in ambush anywhere, and none of them could afford for Starkad to grow reckless. Or more reckless than usual, anyway.

The mine pushed deep underground, every step growing more oppressive. More ... enticing. Despite his better judgment, Starkad's blood raced at the thrill of it.

"This is mist-madness," Gylaug mumbled.

Well ... such words applied to most of Starkad's life. Had

so for a great many years. Thus, what answer could he give the pirate?

They followed the tunnel until it leveled out, and down here, bog water had filtered through. Another tunnel to his left was flooded with foul muck, and even here, Starkad's boots sloshed through it, ankle deep.

Gylaug groaned.

Starkad might have too, though for another reason. Hard to keep quiet when trudging through this. Any chance of stealth was probably lost. And with the muck came the stench of old earth and stagnant waters. They worked through this dankness, the smell growing stronger with every step.

The barest incline, and the muck gave away to actual mud, now squelching beneath his feet. The tunnel opened out into a small chamber where once dvergar or others must have found a deposit, for they had hollowed out a little dome here, supported it with now-rotting boards, one of which had cracked and fallen into two pieces that now stuck up in the mud. Beyond these, Jorund sat in a throne with armrests carved from human skulls.

Starkad had to hand it to the svartalfar. They knew how to make an impression. Even in this foul place—especially in it—the throne cast its occupant as an Otherworldly power, steeped in death and decay, unfathomable to the living. Shadows welled around the throne like a pool of bubbling tar, hissing at their approach.

Jorund rose, hands pressing down on each skull. "At last you come to me."

"Your master is gone from Midgard."

"Indeed. I suppose I ought to thank you for that. Perhaps even grant you a merciful death. But ... sadly ... I have no single drop of mercy in me."

Starkad advanced. "When I'm done, you'll have not a drop of blood left in you."

Jorund smirked, then raised his hands. The shadows around him rose as he did so, the bubbling tar too rose up in tendrils, like a dozen serpents.

If only Hervor would have let him borrow her damned runeblade. It might have proved rather useful, in times like this.

Starkad roared and charged in at Jorund. The svartalf crossed his arms over his chest, and shadow serpents launched themselves at Starkad. He beat them away with his blades, but they forced him to draw his charge up short. Each tendril melted as he struck it, always replaced by another and another rising up out of the darkness. They hissed at him, baring serpent-like fangs and darting in at him from every angle, until he had no choice but to fall back.

Did such shadows carry venom? No way to know, and he could not afford to take the chance they did.

Gylaug joined him at his side, waving his torch—which proved twice as effective as his seax or either of Starkad's swords. The shadow serpents recoiled before the flame even touched them, driven back.

Beyond the shadows, Jorund sneered at them. Every flick of his wrists only intensified the writhing darkness, sending fresh tendrils growing out of them.

"Fall back!" Starkad shouted at Gylaug. "Light more torches while I hold these things back. Light all the torches!"

The pirate did fall back at once.

Roaring, Starkad chopped down serpent after serpent. They grew faster than even he could cut them, though, and he'd be overwhelmed in mere moments.

"Starkad!" Gylaug bellowed.

A bare glance at him.

The pirate waved a torch up and down.

Starkad tossed aside his borrowed sword, and Gylaug flung the torch. This Starkad caught and swung in one motion, driving serpents back. The shadows lurched away, finally letting him reclaim ground.

"Another torch!"

Gylaug raced forward, bearing two more torches, then pressed one at Starkad. After dropping Vikar's sword, Starkad grabbed a second torch from the man. A man could not wield a torch like a sword, exactly, but perhaps like a club. And Starkad had trained with just about every conceivable weapon in his time in Andalus.

Flaming clubs in hand, he twisted, batting serpents aside and turning them to smoke.

Gylaug joined him, the pirate also bearing two torches, and now, snuffing out serpents before they could even finish forming.

Jorund snarled from the darkness, and the torchlight dimmed ... dimmed but did not wink out. Jorund did not have Rathwith's strength or ability to snuff out flame. The svartalf drew his own blade, giving over any attempt to raise more tendrils.

And Starkad had left his swords back in the mud.

No time to go back for them. Instead, he leapt forward, swinging both torches across his chest. The reckless move sent Jorund stumbling away, and Starkad mounted the throne beside him.

Jorund's sword hissed as it parted the air, slashing in at Starkad.

Starkad leapt off the chair and over Jorund. The svartalf's blade cleaved through the armrest and sundered the chair, then came back around to fend off Starkad with uncanny speed.

The fastest man was the only one who mattered.

And right now, without a sword, that was not Starkad.

His torches didn't have the reach or speed of a blade.

Jorund's slashes came with relentless precision. Starkad batted one away. The svartalf smashed his blade through the torch, knocking it from Starkad's hand.

Leaping backward, Starkad whirled the other torch. He edged around, back to where he'd cast aside Vikar's sword.

And Jorund stepped right into the gap. The svartalf knew exactly what Starkad was about, and his vicious, darting blade moved too fast to make a roll for it.

A torch soared end over end and smacked into Jorund's head. The svartalf screamed as his hair caught flame, batting at it with one hand. He dove into the nearest muck pool, rolled around, trying to smother the blaze.

So intent on Starkad, he'd forgotten the pirate.

Starkad raced over, snatched up Vikar's sword, and spun around on Jorund.

Already, Gylaug had jumped down into the muck, sunk in it up to his knees. Screaming, he cleaved at Jorund with his seax. Black blood gushed from a wound he dealt to Jorund's chest.

And then Jorund wrapped a hand around Gylaug's throat and hefted him off his feet. Squeezing.

Starkad charged.

Jorund flung the pirate at him. Unable to help the man, Starkad dove into a roll, and Gylaug collided with the mine wall behind him.

Maybe dead.

Starkad had no time to check.

Jorund had strength and speed born of the Otherworlds.

Starkad had to be faster. He darted in, slashed at Jorund's head. The svartalf parried, off balance but hardly broken. Jorund turned it into a riposte, and Starkad had to parry.

They fell into the dance, back and forth. Muck and mud sloshed about their feet. Both were grunting, heaving.

Jorund lurched forward, tried to snare Starkad with his free hand. Given his superior strength, if he managed that, Starkad was fucked.

Barely twisting out of the way—damned mud sucking at his heels didn't help his mobility—Starkad swung Vikar's sword again. He was too close to use it properly.

Jorund's fist caught him on the side of the head. The blow actually managed to lift him out of the mud, sending him sprawling onto the floor.

Everything spun around him, and Starkad wanted to wretch.

Jorund tromped over toward him, then hesitated. Looked at something. "The traitor ..."

Grunting, Starkad lifted his head.

Wudga was there, Mimung in hand, blood streaming from the blade. The man sniffed. "My father forged this sword beneath Njarar ... forced to it by the cruel King Nidud. Forced into the darkness ... and never able to again set foot into the light. That would have been my urd if not for this man."

"So instead you will die ..."

Wudga shook his head. "Mimung stole the soul of Nidud's own smith to complete its work. Father forged this to avenge the wrongs done to him ... and you have done a great many wrongs, Skafinn."

Skafinn? The svartalf possessing Jorund, maybe.

Starkad pushed himself up.

"You chose a mortal urd," Skafinn said. "And now you

cannot hope to overcome one such as I, blessed with power of the dark, and trained in the sword from ages before your birth."

Wudga sighed. "Perhaps not." He flung Mimung at Starkad's feet.

Skafinn jolted at the thrown weapon, as if he'd first thought Wudga had intended it as a missile.

Starkad snatched up Mimung in his other hand. Its power surged through him. No mortal-wrought blade could equal this one ... and Wudga had trusted Starkad with it.

With a roar, Starkad charged at Skafinn, leading with Vikar's sword. This, the svartalf parried. And Starkad drove Mimung through one of the creature's lungs.

The svartalf's sword toppled out of his fingers as he stared down at the blade embedded in his chest.

Wudga stalked up behind Skafinn and kicked him in the back of the knee, driving the svartalf to the ground. "Every so often, even a mortal is born with a gift."

A gift ... was that what Starkad had? The gift of blood? Of murder?

Well, if that was his gift ... perhaps he had but to use it well.

He jerked Mimung free from Skafinn's chest ... then drove it right through the svartalf's heart.

The creature shuddered and fell limp.

A groan echoed from Gylaug, across the mine. Wudga tromped over to help the pirate up, who soon shook the other man off.

"So," Gylaug said. "I would ask ... that you hang his body from the hall of Upsal. It must stand as a testament that my father ... is avenged."

So much wrought in the name of vengeance. Here, Starkad barely knew this pirate, and he'd come from far

Nidavellir for it. Hervor had fought Jorund to avenge Haki. On and on.

But then, that was only justice.

And if Starkad had a gift, perhaps it was for helping others find their justice. For the justice that Vikar had never found.

Starkad handed Mimung back to Wudga, then looked to Gylaug. "Do with Jorund's body as you wish ... you have earned that right."

36

S lurp!
   The muck squelched as hands tugged Hervor out of it.

With a pained groan, she opened one eye. Ecgtheow had a hand on each of her wrists, pulling her out of the bog.

With a grunt, he released her on dry land—or at least muddy snow. Blood and gore crusted over his mail and had dried in his hair, along his face.

Ecgtheow looked her over, then shook his head and spit. "Lucky I found you, shieldmaiden."

Hervor just groaned. Naught about this day felt lucky.

Orvar was ... still out there.

"So," Ecgtheow said. "We won. Starkad killed Jorund, and Gylaug hung the bastard over there." The big man pointed off toward the stonewall that surrounded the town.

She should have rejoiced at hearing they'd defeated their foe ... should have. If Orvar had not beaten and tortured her within a hairsbreadth of dying. If he had not promised to slowly crush all she cared about in this world.

If he hadn't bitten off her godsdamned finger!

Odin's flaming balls, her hand hurt now that she thought of it.

"Can't walk, huh?" Ecgtheow said. "True but you look like Hel herself shat you out her arse. All right, then." He knelt, hands surprisingly gentle as he slipped them under her neck and waist.

After such a fight, Ecgtheow must have struggled with exhaustion, but he hefted her up like she weighed no more than a child and began to trudge back to the town.

Hervor had never felt so weak, so useless.

Ecgtheow walked halfway there, paused, cracked his neck. Took a few deep breaths. And pressed on. Carried her all the way to the still-smoldering gates.

"I ... can walk from here."

"Sure?"

"Hmmm."

With a grunt, Ecgtheow set her down.

Her legs threatened to give out beneath her. Hervor caught herself on his shoulder, then Ecgtheow slipped his arm around her waist for support. Better than being carried, she supposed.

Like that, she half-walked, half-limped all the way to the Yngling hall. What had once been the Yngling hall. Who knew who would claim it now. In truth, Hervor no longer cared. Orvar had been right ... her vengeance had wrought more blood than she could have begun to imagine. Her careless oath to bring down the slayers of her kin, her oath on Tyrfing. It had brought her here.

And where would Orvar strike next? Her grandfather? Her own town? Or ... Starkad? Ecgtheow? Her few friends ...

Had the draug even driven Jorund to slaughter Haki? Was the king's death on her?

Ecgtheow helped her inside the hall and eased her into a chair that might have once belonged to a queen or thegn.

Such musings were pointless. She was where she was. All she could do was try to find a way forward.

Another shieldmaiden brought her the drinking horn, and she took a swig, then choked as the mead burned her tongue and scorched her throat. She waved away the horn. For the moment, Orvar had robbed her even of the simple pleasures of getting drunk.

Ecgtheow put a hand on her shoulder. "I must speak with Hrethel now, see what he'd have me do next."

Huh. Ecgtheow meant he needed to find out whether Hrethel intended to claim the throne of Upsal for himself. After all, at least two of the petty kingdoms were kingless at the moment, but that was not like to last through the winter.

Someone always slipped into the void.

And Hervor didn't really give a fuck who that was. Her oath was well and truly fulfilled ... so where did that leave her?

Bitter, broken, and alone?

Starkad brushed through the crowd to come stand before her, looked her up and down. He clucked his tongue at what he saw, though he himself looked ragged and worn to the bone.

"I heard you did it ..." she said. Her tongue felt so thick. Her words slurred, like she was drunk. She wished she was drunk, damn it.

Starkad scratched his beard, then looked at his fingers. Given that blood and filth stained his hair, Hervor could imagine what he saw. "Well ... Wudga helped."

"Starkad ... sit with me."

He glanced around, then grabbed a chair and pulled it over. "You did well. Kept the draugar off of me."

Only one draugar truly concerned her at this point. And he needed to know ... Orvar would keep coming for her. Would maybe even come for Starkad. And he needed to know ... that ... that she had murdered his friend.

She opened her mouth, but the words just would not come out. How could they? He might well kill her where she sat. Even if he didn't, he'd never ... never look at her the same again. Never trust her again.

The words churned in her gut, icy and painful. Begging for release they could never find.

She had done it.

She had murdered Orvar-Oddr, even when he had trusted her.

She had become a wretch.

"What is it?" he asked.

Maybe she deserved whatever urd befell her. Even his wrath. For holding it back, keeping the secret, it ate at her. She liked this man ... and lied to him with every breath by the things she could not say.

And she never would.

"I ... I know you," she managed. "You're still going to Glaesisvellir."

Starkad leaned back in his chair, arms folded across his chest. "I'll have to wait until the worst of winter passes before I can chance crossing the Gandvik but yes. I must go ... I have sworn an oath to deliver Skofnung to Gylfi."

For her. He'd given up his prize for her. And now, he would again walk into the vile dangers of the Otherworlds because he could not walk away from an oath made on her behalf. And would Orvar leave him in peace?

Doubtful.

Certainly not once the draug realized Starkad was one of the few people left on Midgard Hervor actually cared about.

Despite herself. Despite the man's arrogant, infuriating ... she shook her head slowly. "You promised to take me with you when you went."

Starkad sniffed, dug his palms at his eyes. "Fuck, Hervor. That was before ... and even then, probably a mistake."

"No. I will not release you from our agreement."

"You have a death wish, woman."

"Do you?"

Starkad flinched. Was that ... was she closer to the mark than she'd expected? Did part of him *want* to die? He spent nigh to every waking moment chasing adventure and treasure and fame, and doing it oft at the most dangerous extremes of the world imaginable. Beyond this world, even.

Cursed to live a long life, alone, and ever unsatisfied.

Hervor glowered. Well, she wouldn't let him face it alone. Not Glaesisvellir, not Orvar, not any of it.

"The winter ..." She cleared her throat. "It will give us time to heal. Give you more time ... to help me master left-handed fighting."

He groaned. "You will not change your mind?"

No. And her eyes must have told him that, for he nodded, patted her knee, and rose.

Glowering, she watched him go, out into the throng, perhaps seeking drink as he so oft did.

So ... the better part of a single winter to find her strength ... to learn to be all she'd once been.

And to be ready to head off, beyond the bounds of Midgard.

A chill wracked her.

EPILOGUE

Odin's back ached as he trod back to Volund's workshop. Tracking the smith down in Sviarland had proved fruitless, but Odin had known the svartalf would have to return here, sooner or later.

No surprise, then, that hammer blows once again greeted his arrival.

This time, though, Volund paused mid-stroke and let the hammer drop to his side. A fell gleam lit his eyes as he turned to look upon Odin.

"Another visit?"

Odin strode closer, until he stood just across the anvil. This he rapped with Gungnir and shook his head. "I warned you to tread with care around Starkad."

Volund shrugged. "Eightarms lives."

"Barely."

"Strength is forged through suffering. Perhaps you should thank me. Perhaps even request I continue ... the tortures the dvergar wrought onto me make Starkad's pains seem pale and hardly worth mentioning."

Odin glowered. "You did not do this for his benefit.

Indeed, I find myself ... suspecting all that happened was a scheme to weaken Prince Rathwith. Cast out of this world, the vaettr must now find his hold on the courts of Svartalfheim precarious. Perhaps thus giving more maneuvering room to his sister's bastard son."

Volund flashed a toothy grin. "I have no idea what you mean, King of the Aesir."

Odin nodded. "Or perhaps you thought you could win regardless of the outcome. If Rathwith claimed all Sviarland as his domain, he'd have you to thank for it, and your fortunes must rise with his. If he failed ... well then, someone else would have the chance to step up and claim what he'd lost."

"Huh. That sounds like an excellent plan. I wish I'd thought of it."

Odin surged strength into his limbs, lunged forward. Grabbed the anvil with one hand and flung it, spinning, crashing over the floor.

Volund fell back a step, hammer raised as if the tool might stand a mere instant against Gungnir. Against Odin's wrath.

But Odin paused. Blew out a long breath. He still *needed* Volund to finish his works. Without this treacherous alf, all the worlds might fall before Hel. "There is a flaw in your schemes, my friend. If Rathwith had succeeded in possessing Starkad, you might not have come out so far ahead as you seem to think. You would have found me rather ... *displeased*."

"But. He did. *Not*."

Odin shook his head and took several steps backward. Without Volund, he might never see Freyja again. Even the whole world might fall in Ragnarok. And *still*, he was tempted to strike him down, here and now.

"This is your last warning to stay away from Starkad, Volund. I need the other runeblades back in play, and I need Starkad to get them."

Volund snorted. "Peace, Ás. I have no further interest in your pawn. And I rather think he will now move on to Glaesisvellir seeking Skofnung. That is what you wanted, is it not?"

"Of course he will go to Glaesisvellir." Odin turned from the smith.

Wherever rumors of a runeblade lurked, Starkad would go. Of course he would ... he had no choice.

Such was the urd Odin had set upon him.

A fate pulled from darkness, years ago.

The Saga continues in *Days of Frozen Hearts:*

http://books2read.com/daysfrozen

SKALDS' TRIBE

Join the Skalds' Tribe and get access to exclusive reader rewards like *The Ragnarok Era Codex*, as well getting free books like *Darkness Forged* and notifications on release dates and sales.

https://www.mattlarkinbooks.com/go-runeblade/

Want maps, character bios, and background information on the Ragnarok Era? Look no further.

DAYS OF FROZEN HEARTS EXCERPT

*A*fter passing the winter here, the Yngling hall at Upsal had almost started to feel like home. Strange thought, given that Hervor had sworn an oath to bring down the Ynglings at any cost. And here she was, sipping mead and leaning back against the table, cheering the spectacle with the rest of them.

Benches had been pushed aside in the center of the hall, making way for the contestants. Ecgtheow the Tiny had both arms locked around Starkad, bearing him down to the ground. It looked like the big man was finally going to pin his opponent. Despite all Starkad's speed, Ecgtheow was larger and stronger than ... well, almost anyone.

Ecgtheow grunted, driving Starkad down. Starkad tilted over backward. As he did so, he twisted around so fast Hervor barely followed. Suddenly Ecgtheow was in midair, flipping over Starkad's shoulder. Hervor's mouth fell open the instant before the big man hit the dusty ground. A horrendous *oomph* escaped Ecgtheow and the man lay dazed.

Huh. Hervor had trained at wrestling since she was

seven winters old. By the time she was nine, she could beat boys her age, a few even older than her. She still couldn't have pulled off what Starkad just had. The man never ceased to amaze.

King Aun raised his drinking horn. "Eightarms!" The others echoed his cheer throughout the hall. Everyone was in good spirits, what with summer now underway. Summer meant time for crops and safer fishing and, of course, raids. Well ... except Aun refused to send his people raiding. The new Yngling king claimed Upsal had lost enough men in the wars.

Man was a craven, no doubt. These Ynglings were like weeds. Yngvi and Alf were dead. Alf's son Ochilaik was dead. Yngvi's sons Jorund and Eikkr were dead. Hervor had helped most of them to the grave. And now here was Aun, some cousin to the slain who popped up in the western reaches of Upsal, almost into Dalar.

Man had come to claim the throne when there was no one left alive to challenge him.

Maybe Hervor ought to have killed him too, but ... She'd already held her oath fulfilled.

So much blood.

Yngvi's man had slain Hervor's father, but she'd killed the murderer and the king's son both. What more could Father expect from her? Was she to scour every snowy mound and bog in Sviarland to make sure not a single Yngling pest survived?

No, she had seen enough of war in any event. War had cost her friends, family, even her own body ... her right arm might never again be as strong as it had been. She'd spent the past moons trying to heal, trying to train to fight left-handed.

And by Odin's balls, that was an ordeal.

Besides, she'd given her *new* oath to Starkad, promised to help the man recover a runeblade from Jotunheim. Odin preserve her against such folly.

AUTHOR'S RAMBLINGS

The Ynglings are the most famous of the Swedish dynasties, maybe of all the Scandinavian dynasties. Snorri wrote substantially about them in his *Heimskringla* (basically a chronicle of stories about the Norse kings, the first section of which is the *Yngling Saga*). For my work, I condensed some of these stories a bit to ensure they could unfold in a manner conducive to the structure of a novel.

Nevertheless, a small chunk of the stories of the Ynglings forms the foundations of the political aspects of this book. Hervor's role in the events mythologically is small, merely intersecting with them through the Tyrfing Cycle, but I saw no reason not to maintain her as the central character here.

Starkad, naturally, does appear frequently through these tales, showing up at decisive battles over several generations. As far as his background story, I derived that mainly from the *Gautreks Saga* and the *Hervarar Saga* (i.e., *The Saga of King Heidrik*, the same tale from which Hervor comes).

Within my work, we see the earliest foundations of Starkad's background begin in *The Mists of Niflheim* (*The Ragnarok Era*, book 2) and continue into *The Shores of Vana-*

heim (book 3). Starkad's first flashbacks in this book take place a few years after *Shores* ends.

Obviously, *Days of Bloody Thrones* also serves as a rough sequel or continuation of Volund's tale, which I began in *Darkness Forged*. Volund gets his revenge in *Darkness Forged* but lets Otwin live for decades more, mainly because of the son he impregnated Bodvild with (Wudga). We get the impression Volund may have been subtly encouraging Wudga down this path for a while, but it all comes to a head when Volund sends Wudga to hire his old friend Starkad.

I think this book has a similar tone to *Darkness Forged*, in that it's even darker than *Days of Endless Night*. This darkness was necessary for the tale, but it did prove emotionally challenging to write. There is a great deal of anger and hatred going on in the world, both as people relate to one another, and as they relate to the Otherworlds (the supernatural). In order to be meaningful, this hatred has to manifest in inhumane and even inhuman ways, with the ghost world doing the most awful things imaginable to people.

The Ragnarok Era series itself sometimes flirted with horror aspects, and the nature of the *Runeblade Saga* brings these books closer to being true horror/fantasy in addition to sword and sorcery adventures. This combination is dear to my heart—I find it compelling, with a strong precedent in works like *Conan* and *Elric*—so I hope it provided an enjoyable read.

Finally, I want to extend a big thanks to my developmental editor, Clark, for helping me work through the complex outline and structure for this series. Thanks to my family for their support, and to my copyeditor and cover designer for helping me create a polished final product.

Thank you for reading,

Matt

P.S. Reviews are super important, especially to small presses like mine. Without reviews, small presses cannot get ads. It takes only a single line or two to make that difference. So if you liked this, please leave a review where you bought it!

Want to talk about the book? I'd love to hear from you. You can reach me at: matt@incandescentphoenix.com

BOOKS BY MATT LARKIN

The Ragnarok Era

The Ragnarok Era is a dark fantasy retelling of Norse mythology, chronicling Odin's rise to godhood. If you love old legends, tragic mythology, and action-packed reads, check out The Ragnarok Era now!

http://www.mattlarkinbooks.com/ragnarok/

Legends of the Ragnarok Era

Legends of the Ragnarok Era expands on the world developed in The Ragnarok Era series by delivering dark tales outside the main series narrative. Fans of mythology should not miss this epic series.

http://www.mattlarkinbooks.com/ragnaroklegend/

Runeblade Saga

The Runeblade Saga is a series of dark fantasy sword and sorcery adventures set in the world of The Ragnarok Era. Filled with plenty of grim action, tragic heroes, and more than a bit of horror, these books are for fans of mythology and sword & sorcery alike.

http://www.mattlarkinbooks.com/runeblade/

For my wife and daughter.

Made in the USA
Columbia, SC
21 April 2020